ARCANE SOULS
WORLD

ERRORS AND EXORCISMS

THE WRONG WITCH
BOOK THREE

ANNIE ANDERSON

ERRORS & EXORCISMS

Arcane Souls World

The Wrong Witch Book 3

International Bestselling Author

Annie Anderson

Edited by Angela Sanders

Cover Design by Trif Book Designs

www.annieande.com

For my readers. Thanks for the wild ride.

The Moon will guide you through the night with her brightness, but she will always dwell in the darkness in order to be seen.

— SHANNON L. ALDER

THREE YEARS AGO

In-laws really were the worst.

Sure, most people had clashes in personality, the odd conflict here and there, but me? I got the raw end of the deal when it came to my wife's family. Then again, Wren could have probably said the same shit about mine—and she'd have been right, considering the throat-slitting event at our first family dinner.

But at present, she wasn't dealing with homicidal witches hell-bent on eviscerating her from the inside out, and I was, so...

When I woke up this morning with Wren in my arms, I never thought my day would end like this. We were supposed to make sure she was ready to go to the

ABI. We were supposed to laugh and joke and make love and go to bed and wake up tomorrow and do it all over again.

I wasn't supposed to run all over Savannah, trying not to get us both killed.

I wasn't supposed to realize we both wouldn't make it out of here.

I wasn't supposed to tell my best friend to take her away from me.

I wasn't supposed to tell her goodbye.

I wouldn't trade it now. Because Wren was safe, and these women would never touch her again—as long as I could hold them back.

Dodging the blade, I nearly ran into Wren's cracked-out mother, who was doing her level best to electrocute me to death. All things considered, I was pegging Wren's family as the raw end of the deal. Especially since they were the reason I was never going to see her again.

"What's the matter, Fido?" Margot simpered as she clutched a crackling ball of power in her palm. "You afraid of a little shock?"

A shock? No.

Getting roasted from the inside out? Absolutely.

Several decades my senior, the Bannister witches could make me a stain on the floor if I gave them the chance. It wasn't like our families had ever gotten along, but ever since Eloise Bannister found out I was married to her granddaughter, I'd known my days were numbered.

I just didn't think it would be this soon.

I thought I had more time—I thought *we* had more time.

Wren's Aunt Judith—who could definitely pass for a ginger Bellatrix Lestrange—slashed at me with a knife that reeked of poison. The wicked blade missed my skin by millimeters, stealing all my attention as a ball of electricity slammed into my shoulder.

I'd never been tased before, but if I had a guess, it felt just like this. The jolt surged through my body, frying neurons as it locked my muscles, nearly making me stumble.

Judith's blade slashed again, biting into my feeble forearm, still weak from the shock.

Fuck.

Acid-like poison snaked up my arm, its toxic fingers blackening the skin as I made a cut of my own.

I wouldn't let these women go after Wren. I'd made my peace with the fact that I wouldn't get forever with the woman I loved. Decided as soon as I let Wyatt take Wren out of here, that I wasn't going to make it. So this poison being my undoing? Well, it was expected.

But I'd be taking both of them with me.

My claws made a home in Judith's belly, and I ripped upward, tearing her middle wide. Shock colored her pale features that were so close to Wren's. But Judith was sadistic and cold—her sister no better—and I wasn't sorry she was going to die in this room right alongside me.

Margot howled, firing off more orbs of magic, but I used Judith as a shield, letting her take the brunt of the hits. The scent of ozone, spent magic, and burning flesh ran rank through the room, singeing my nostrils in the process. I was lucky I was dying or else I'd never get that smell out of my nose.

And I *was* dying. The poison had made my left arm useless, and standing was becoming a real problem.

But over the scent of Judith's burning flesh and the poison rotting me from the inside out, and over Margot screams, and the strobing lights of the magic, there was something else. Flashes hit my brain, but unlike the first time they'd knocked me for a loop, I knew exactly what they were. I was seeing through Wren's eyes, the mate bond giving me this small glimpse of her before I wouldn't see anything else ever again.

But then the scent of mage filled my nose and the woman in my arms flickered out and disappeared.

Margot faded to nothing, and the black fingers of death cleared from my veins.

Lies. All lies.

My wolf howled in my brain as more visions of Wren filled my head. Her heart raced in my chest, her fear. She was looking at Wyatt, but his face was melting away, another man standing in his place.

Illusion mage. It was all fake.

My gut bottomed out as my feet finally got with the program. I was out the French doors and over the wall before I even realized I was moving, following the scent of Wren and the mage.

How could I have been so stupid? They had never been here. Wyatt had never been here. I let some asshole take my wife right out from under my nose. It had all been a fucking ploy to get Wren away from me— get her to a Fae gate. That poor agent had family, probably. Family far stronger than she was.

The square across the street held several Fae gates. All it would take was opening a door.

I burst from the trees, only to see Wren struggling against the hold of an impossibly tall man, his hunched frame doing nothing to hide his size. He was thin as a rail, and he had hands on my woman.

"Let me go," Wren screeched, planting her feet as he tried pulling her toward the door.

But as much as I wanted to look at her, my gaze was locked on the man watching the tableau as if he were bored out of his mind. Blackness coated his fingers, the oily darkness like a death mage, but not all at the same time. Plus, he didn't smell right—not mage, not witch, not warlock.

No, he was a Fae.

A dark one, my wolf supplied, knowing far more about the liminal spaces than I did. I had to get her free.

Had to.

"Wren," I roared, and those gorgeous green-gold eyes met mine.

And then I knew.

There was nothing I wouldn't do to get to her.

No blood I wouldn't spill.

No one I wouldn't kill.

My wolf took over, jumping free of my skin, pumping my legs faster. We had to get to her, we had to move, we had to fight.

The Fae in black sighed, his boredom getting the better of him as he shot putrid darkness from his hand, the blackness so thick it was like a wall separating me from Wren. I lunged, trying to get through, but it was like ramming into stone.

I could barely see through the murky smoke, but I could still make out Wren's struggle.

"Nico," she pleaded, right before the lanky man wrenched her through the door and it slammed closed.

The dark one fisted his hand, and the door disappeared, almost as if the portal itself had been erased. Then, it felt as if my heart had been ripped from my chest. I couldn't feel Wren's mind, her emotions were just gone. I'd never been able to explain just what feeling her all the time was like, but it was as if everything about the woman I loved was cold and dead, stolen from my very being as if someone had sucked out my soul.

Tossing my head back, I howled, my wolf calling for a moon that was not there—for a pack that was not mine, for a love lost to me. But a wolf's howl did more than just call for aid, it was a magic all on its own. The blackness shivered, rippling into spikes as my wolf bade the whole of Savannah for help.

"Stop that," the pompous fuck of a Fae shouted, one hand covering his ear as he tried to hold me back.

My wolf completed its call before snapping at the Fae, ready and willing to take a chunk out of him the first chance we got.

The Fae fisted his hands as he threw his arms wide, his dark eyes alighting with his magic as they turned a very odd shade of blue. Black magic grew, the pressure of it nearly bringing me to my knees as it pressed on the very air around me.

It stole the breath from my lungs, leaving me gasping on the grass, praying for help.

"Look," the Fae bit out, his British accent thick. "I don't want to do this, but my father has left me no choice. The only way to stop him is to keep him from crossing into this plane. If I have to sacrifice one girl to do it, so fucking be it. I know she's your sweetheart and all, but letting that girl stay will be the end of us all. At least this way she'll take care of a real problem before she wipes us all out."

The darkness faded, but the pressure squeezing the life out of me didn't let up for a second as he knelt by my shoulder.

"If we're lucky, you'll never see that girl again." He cocked his head to the side as if he were studying me. "I doubt you'll see it my way, but trust me on this one, mate. That girl will be the end of us all. But, since I can't have you following me—"

The pressure eased for half a second—just long enough for me to catch a breath—before his fist knocked right into my temple.

And my last thought before the light dimmed was of Wren.

"Are you going to tell him, or am I?" my mother hissed, her voice as quiet as a whisper but still felt louder than a fucking drum knocking against my skull.

Maybe it wasn't a drum. Maybe it was a jackhammer. If I didn't know better, I'd think someone had taken a baseball bat to my head.

I cracked a single eyelid and instantly regretted it. I hadn't had a hangover this bad since that one time Theo had taken me to spring break in Miami when I was seventeen. My hold on my wolf had been very new, and I hadn't figured out the healing bit yet. Healing myself from the alcohol poisoning had been a treat.

"What happened?" I croaked, trying to sit up. The only way to do this was to just get it done. I needed carbs, grease, and enough red meat to choke a goat. Then I'd be right as rain.

But something felt off. I was in my bed at the pack house. I shouldn't be at the pack house. Why would I when I hadn't slept here in weeks. Why...

Then it all came flooding back. The running, the fighting, the beautiful woman stolen from me.

Wren.

I shot off the bed, staggering as my head swam and my stomach pitched. My legs nearly folded beneath me, but I held onto one of the bedposts like my life depended on it. It didn't, but hers did.

"What. Happened," I ordered, the Alpha emerging from my voice in such a way that had Dayana shivering and Mari's gaze hitting the floor. It didn't matter if I was hurt. That Alpha power was enough to back me up.

But neither of them answered me. No, it was my mother who looked me in the eye and filled me in. "We heard your call and came to find you. You were in Chatham Square. Bloody, unconscious, barely breathing. Smelling of Fae. The bastard nearly caved in your skull. The boys helped me bring you here."

I'd get into the fact that my mother had my brothers bring me here of all places later. What I wanted to know is what she didn't want to tell me.

If she wouldn't cough it up, I'd start. "Wren's gone —taken—to the Fae realm. The one you smell, kept me from her. Anyone catch his trail?"

And there was no way they couldn't smell him. The scent of his magic was all over me, nearly making me puke.

Mom nodded, but Mari spoke. "Theo and Mateo are out scouting—" At my censuring glare, she held up a hand. "They wanted to make amends for what they did.

Santi and Frankie are rounding up Wren's friends. Making sure they're safe."

I had a very bad feeling about this. There was no way my brothers would be out scouting or helping me after what they had done—after my father's behavior —unless... Unless something was wrong with Dad. Unless there was another Acosta problem. No one would defy the Alpha unless they didn't have an Alpha anymore.

"What aren't you telling me?" Because they were leaving shit out, and if I wanted to find Wren—which I sure as fuck did—then I'd need their help.

My older sister Lara waltzed into the room, her pregnant belly leading the way as she munched on pita chips from a massive bag. Each crunch rattled my skull.

"A lot, little brother. First off, Mom challenged Dad and won." *Crunch.* "He's in the dungeon pacing like a caged animal right now, and honestly, I love this for him. Then she reprimanded Theo for putting a blade to your mate's throat—dick move by the way—and forced him to give up his pack second status, took his house, and made him pay two million in restitution. You should really check your bank account more." *Crunch.* "After that, Mom excommunicated Diana, stripped her of Acosta protection, and let the Savannah Arcane Council have her for attempted murder of a packmate."

She turned to Mom, nibbling on another chip. "Did I forget anything?"

Mom rolled her eyes as she straightened the already-perfect duvet. "Now is not the time for this, Lara. Nico needs to rest and—"

"*Mom.*"

But she wouldn't meet my gaze, instead her lip trembled. "It's bad, sweetheart. There's a lot going on and you're still not in fighting shape. I've done what I can, but I'm not the Alpha. Your father was, and even though I won the challenge... We need you, okay?"

But did they? I couldn't even keep my mate safe, and they wanted me to take my father's place? What good was I going to do?

Mom shook her head as she began wringing her hands—a bad sign if there ever was one. Mom's wringing of hands was the equivalent to the Joint Chiefs calling Defcon One. "The witches are in an uproar demanding Wren be returned to them. There's been disturbances within the pack, and some wolves are miss—"

My body went on red alert when Fiona strode into the room like she'd been here a thousand times before. If her light-blonde hair weren't a complete mess or her lip split, she'd be the picture of composure. But she didn't give me a second to ask why she was bleeding or why my brother Santi was walking in behind her with a black eye, a busted nose, and a limp.

"What your mama is skirting around is all the Fae portals in the city are locked up tighter than a duck's asshole, the River Walk is in a tizzy, the ABI is breathing down our necks trying to recall us all, and they need you to sack up an—"

Wren. If the Fae portals were closed, how was I supposed to get her back? How was I going to breathe? A sharp pain knifed through my chest as I struggled to suck in air.

"What I need to do is find my fucking wife."

The blood on my father's office floor was brown with age. No one had bothered to clean it up since I'd held Wren in my arms, her throat pouring scarlet lifeblood as her heart fluttered and stopped. His desk was in shambles, the bookcases torn apart with books and papers scattered over the floor as if there had been a war.

Maybe because there had been.

I'd faced down not only my family, but Death herself in this room, and luckily, she'd been kind—giving Wren back to me, allowing me to bring the woman I loved back from the brink.

But how lucky had I really been?

I rubbed at the ache in my chest, the stitch there wasn't getting any better, each breath no easier than the last. It was as if I was missing a limb. A huge chunk of me was just... gone. I'd gotten so used to feeling Wren in every single cell of my body, inured to her emotions, her heartbeat, her breaths, that to have them absent felt like I had lost myself in that gods-damned gate.

But I'd get her back—even if I had to tear this world and the next apart in the trying.

"Nic?"

The absolute last person I wanted to talk to was my eldest brother.

Not now.

Not in this room.

Not with Wren gone.

Not ever.

If I were steady on my feet—if this ache in my chest wasn't ripping me apart with every fucking breath—I would have honored the promise I made him. But ripping Theo limb from limb wasn't a possibility now. I would just ignore him, and if the fucker was smart, he would turn his ass around and never talk to me again.

But my brother wasn't smart. Never had been.

Theo's hand on my shoulder had me whipping around, my fist slamming into his jaw without my brain ever telling it to move. All I could think about was that gods-damned knife to Wren's perfect throat. His hands on her. His will to do her harm.

Theo fell to the floor, hands up, mouth bloody, his pleading expression doing nothing but making my teeth grind. But though I expected him to move, he did not. He didn't say a word. All he did was stay right there on that filthy floor and look at me like if I killed him, I'd be doing him a favor.

"What do you want?" I seethed through gritted teeth, aching to take this pain out on someone—anyone else. Someone had to feel as bad as I did. Someone had to have this ache. Someone had to have every single breath in their lungs feel like acid.

His huff of laughter was completely mirthless. "To keep you from feeling like I bet you are right now. That's what I want. It's enough to make you crazy, isn't it? That ache in your chest that just won't go away? The feeling like something is missing? Like you're dying but the universe is just too cruel to actually do you that favor?"

But if anyone knew how I felt, it was Theo, wasn't it? His mate had died before he'd been able to find her—killed before her time, before *their* time. A pit of dread yawned wide in my gut, threatening to swallow me whole.

"Please tell me it always felt like this, and not..."

Please tell me you felt this ache always.

Please don't tell me you only felt it after your mate died.

Wren can't be dead. Please, Fates, don't tell me she's…

The ache in my chest intensified, biting through me as if the claws of the devil himself were reaching inside and ripping my soul from my body. I'd never understood Theo. Never understood why he was such a dick, why he hated everyone, why he refused to be around us if he could help it. Pack houses were meant to be filled to the brim, bursting with mates and children and life. But ours wasn't. So many of our pack lived without mates, outside of the pack house, away from the bustle of children and happy couples and reminders of what they didn't have.

Theo's expression did not waver. He held that pleading look like he was trying to hide the pity. Either that or he just didn't want to die. "It's always felt like I was being ripped in two. I haven't known a day of peace since she graced this planet and not a single one since she left it."

My brother was over a century old. A century of days filled with agony. Maybe him not wanting to die was a stretch. The thought of centuries without Wren was getting harder and harder to swallow.

"She's not dead, brother," Theo urged, his tone soft even though his face was not. "Your woman has far too much fight in her to let some pissant Fae take her down. She's an Alpha. Like you. Wolf or not."

My lip curled at his patronizing. Leave it to Theo to try and stroke my ego while he was bloody and flat on his back. "Pretty words won't save you from me. Not after what you did."

Again, Theo's chuckle was mirthless. "Do you think I had a choice, brother? Unlike you, the rest of us aren't Alphas. We *can't* say no."

He shook his head as he rolled, getting to his knees as he stared at me with an expression of disgust so powerful it made me wonder if I'd ever known Theo at all. If I'd ever known my father.

"I knew how wrong it was—how wrong we all were—the second she begged for your life. The moment Wren begged me to protect you, I knew Dad was wrong. That what we were doing wasn't the right path. But he'd been so blinded by Diana's premonition that he couldn't see just how much Wren loves you. But when she pleaded with me, I knew." Helpless tears filled his eyes before they found the floor. "But the order had been given, and I couldn't say no. Then again, wrong or right, I wasn't planning on leaving the room alive, so the consequences didn't matter, now, did they?"

That had me stumbling back a step. "You thought I'd kill you."

Had I considered it? Absolutely. But the reality of

actually murdering my brother was far too big a pill to swallow.

Theo's gaze never left the floor as his shoulders rounded forward, his body sagging just a little. "I was hoping for it, actually. Too bad your honor's better than mine, isn't it?"

The truth was, had Wren died that day, my honor would have evaporated. There wouldn't have been anything good left in me. She would have taken it all with her.

Funny, I'd gotten a reprieve, but now I knew that the ugly side of myself was closer to the surface than it had ever been. Because she was gone and all I wanted to do was rip this world apart to get her back.

"Is it?" I growled, my wolf so close to the surface it was as if he were the one clawing to get out. "Tell me, brother—do you still want to die?"

Theo's shoulders straightened, his eyes finally meeting mine, his expression more of the brother I knew from my childhood before life decided to kill his soul. "Maybe later. I have things to attend to. Like helping you find your woman."

Theo and Matteo had been on the trail of the Fae who'd kept me from Wren. A dark one. A Dark Fae, maybe? My wolf had been a little sketchy on the details, and even as close to the surface as he was, the damn animal was still mum on the subject.

"You didn't find the Fae, did you?"

My brother clenched his jaw as his gaze slid back to the ground. "We were close, but *he* called us back. Used the pack bond and…" Theo shook his head, his whole body vibrating with rage. "Mom might have won the challenge, but you and I both know Dad let her win because his wolf wouldn't let him kill his own mate and any other outcome would demand it. He's still Alpha. Unless someone takes him down, he's going to undermine everything he can so he can steal his seat back. Matteo and I were in fucking Kentucky when he—"

Theo swallowed hard, bending forward so his head was damn near on the ground. "I failed you, brother. I accept whatever fate you wish to dole out."

The bond I had to this pack had been severed days ago, but I still knew what my father had done. Taking someone's will away was not a favorite tool of mine, but for some, it was commonplace. Dad hadn't used that Alpha power much—at least not with me—but something inside me told me that this wasn't the first time he'd bent Theo to his will. No, my father might never have been who I thought he was.

And now he'd let Wren's trail go cold. On purpose.

That fucking bastard.

The stoked embers of all the pain and rage and loss in my gut burned bright as my wolf clawed at my mind.

"Look at me and tell me the truth," I ordered, threading every bit of Alpha into my voice as I knelt to stare my brother in the eye. "Did he take your will the night Wren almost died?"

I knew the answer already, but I needed to hear it from his lips. I needed to know if my father was unfit for leadership. I needed it unquestioned and concrete.

And I needed to know now.

"In what world would I steal another's mate from them otherwise? He fed us lies and stole our will— believing Diana's prophecy rather than his own son." Theo's gaze fell to the floor. "I'm sorry for the part I played and the damage I caused. I don't have the strength to leave on my own like you do. But if you'll have me, I will fight for you until my last breath."

We'd have to circle back to Diana's prophecy, but I had a sinking feeling it had something to do with what the dark one had said after closing the gates to the Fae realm.

I doubt you'll see it my way, but trust me on this one, mate. That girl will be the end of us all.

Did I give a fuck what Diana saw or what that bastard said?

Absolutely fucking not.

Because whatever she saw, it had nothing to do with my Wren. Wren couldn't be the end of anyone or anything. Not unless they crossed her, and then it wouldn't be her bringing their end.

It would be me.

I stood, grabbing my brother's hand and yanking him to his feet. Pulling him close, I whispered nothing but the truth in his ear.

"When I get Wren back, you so much as look at her sideways and I'll gut you like a fish for the entire pack to see. Understand?"

Relief relaxed my brother's shoulders as he brought me in for a hug. "I would expect nothing less. And I'll expect her punishment when she returns as well. I know we aren't square, but I'll do my best to make it up to you both."

Squeezing him tight, I felt a minor hint of relief until the reality of what I'd have to do hit me like a ton of bricks. Theo wanted to be in my pack if I ever made one. He wanted help leaving. Well, he wouldn't have to go far.

If I wanted every resource to find Wren, if I wanted to keep my father from undermining every move, every effort, if I wanted my brothers to never have their will taken away again, I'd have to do the thing I'd been dreading for decades.

Because there was only room for one Acosta Alpha.

I released Theo, slapping him on the back so he knew I heard him. "Keep Mom busy, will you? I have to go handle some business."

Theo's face went gray for a second before he nodded. "I'll stay with her until... until the end."

Gritting my teeth, I directed my feet to the door, following them to the one place I did not want to go. That was the thing about being Alpha that my father forgot. Sometimes it wasn't about what you wanted to do.

Sometimes it was about what you *had* to do.

Savannah should not have dungeons of any kind. Being on the coast, the water table was obnoxiously high. Luckily, the arcane world was sometimes kind. A few centuries before I was born, this home had been retrofitted with tunnels and a cave system, and of course, the dungeon.

I never understood why anyone would build a dungeon in a shifter den. We didn't keep prisoners. Wolves were known to cut out the middleman and just take our enemies out altogether. If someone would have asked me a month ago if my father would ever be on my list of enemies, I'd have called them crazy.

Now? Not so much.

What else could the man be? He'd tried to have

Wren killed. He'd called Theo and Matteo back from Wren's trail. He'd intervened, took my brothers' will away, and destroyed our pack. If any other Alpha had done what my father had, the question as to whether or not they'd live to see tomorrow would be an easy one to answer.

"Finally come to see your old man, huh?" my father asked from the floor of the damp dungeon cell. A putrid bucket filled with something foul sat in the corner and Dad appeared to not have eaten in several days. The eyes of his wolf burned in the darkness, his sunken cheeks and eviscerated frame leaning listlessly against the bars. The magic in the metal smoldered bright, searing his flesh through his shirt, but still my father never flinched.

Maybe it was because of the arm hanging half-gone at his side, or maybe it was the still-wide-open- and bleeding wounds at his middle. Wounds that smelled worse than the bucket. Jesus fuck, what had Mom done to him?

"Was that your goal?" I swallowed down bile, my gut churning with all that I didn't want to do. "To make me come down here and deal with you?"

Because there was no way my mother would have the strength to kill Dad. They'd been together for centuries. Killing him had never been an option. But she wanted me to be Alpha, and there was only one way to do it.

"Come on, son. You and I both know how this is going to go. All I have to do is make you mad enough, and you'll handle the situation. You've always been a hothead."

But it was tough to find my rage, especially as the scent of death filled the air.

"Your wolf won't heal you," I murmured, guessing the situation almost immediately. "Because you went against your mate—against your pack—and now you're facing the consequences."

I'd heard of our animals doing this, but I'd only ever seen it in the lore, not in practice.

And never to an Alpha.

"She's going to bring the end to us all, Nicholas. I was protecting my family. What else would you have me do?"

This was the second time I'd heard this supposed "end of the world" claim, and honestly, I was getting sick of it.

"Wren will do no such thing. She is my wife, which makes her your fucking family, too. Where was her protection? Where was your care for your son? Where was the fucking proof, other than the word of one old woman?"

"Diana has prevented more war and more blood-shed than your small mind can even comprehend, boy."

Weak. My father was weak and small and...

"At what cost? Sometimes, blood needs to be spilled. Sometimes wars need to be fought. And sometimes the word of your son is more important than that of an old seer aching for death. You tore your family apart at her word, took your sons' will away. You broke us. The Acosta bond is weaker because of you."

My father's wolf burned bright in his eyes once again, but something was different this time. Dad wasn't in control of his animal anymore. No, it was separate, other, his wolf aching—clawing—to come out. It called to me, beckoned me to use just a little bit of the power Wren had shared with me—that same power that made me almost positive she was still alive, still breathing, still able to come back to me.

"I was going to wait for Wren to decide your punishment, but we both know you won't last that long. This is only going to go down one of two ways. One, I let your wolf do what he wanted and let you fester and die in this fucking cell. Two, I rip your wolf right out of your skin and snap your insidious neck with a mercy you don't deserve."

I tried to reconcile the man before me with the one who helped me during my first shift. The same man that taught me to drive and be a man and an Alpha. How could he be the same person?

How could he do all that and be the man who took his sons' will away?

Dad—*Tomás*—tried and failed to sit up, his eyes wide. "There's no way you can do that. Only Spirit Alphas can even attempt something li—" He hissed in pain, clutching his middle. "Nicholas, this changes everything. Diana doesn't know what you are. Her prophecy is wro—"

But he hadn't put it together. Diana knew I could heal Wren before she ever sliced that blade. She'd just hoped I wasn't up to the task. And Spirit Alphas were a fucking myth—dreamed up by some seer ages ago. It was why my being able to heal others was so dicey. There were enough prophecies about Spirit Alphas to fill a gods-damned library, and any one of them could get me killed if the wrong person knew about me.

"She knows," I growled, cutting him off. "The problem you aren't seeming to grasp is that Diana is not serving anyone but Diana—a fact you should have caught onto as soon as she suggested killing my wife."

Bile rose in my throat. The only reason he was still alive was because no one wanted to be the one to kill him. Mom didn't want to kill her mate. Theo didn't have the strength, Ella wasn't an Alpha, and Mariella was too young.

But me?

The only reason Tomás was still alive was all due to the woman he wanted dead. I couldn't kill my father in front of Wren.

But Wren wasn't here, now, was she?

"I won't have you interfering again, old man. No more controlling your pack. No more taking their will away."

"No, son. You don't understand—"

But I didn't let him finish. There wasn't anything he could say to me that would change his fate any more than it would change mine. Drawing on the power Wren had once shared with me, I closed my fist on the air itself and pulled, yanking my father's wolf from his skin. Blindingly white just like Theo, the animal jumped from the liminal space under my father's skin, severing the tie between the two.

Spirit Alphas were a myth, but then again, so was what I had just done. It had been said that they could heal or destroy, and as much as I hated it, destroying felt really fucking good right about then.

My father gasped as his skin grayed out, losing far more blood now that his wolf was no longer connected to him. He choked, trying to talk, and it reminded me so much of Wren dying in my arms that I fought back a snarl.

Without anything blocking my way, I opened the cell door to stand over him.

"See that feeling you have right now? That's the same one my wife felt when Diana slit her fucking throat." Tilting my head, I knelt at his side, realizing that this man wasn't anything to me—not anymore. "Lucky for you, I'm kinder than you were."

Tomás' eyes widened just a little, but his expression was resolute as my claws dug into the flesh of his throat and ripped it wide. Ten seconds later, my father took his last breath. Two seconds after that, the full weight of the Acosta line fell on my shoulders, the power hitting me like a ton of bricks.

Staggering to my feet, I let it fill me, let it heal the last of the aches... all except that one in my heart.

That was here to stay.

Turning my attention to the very large, very wild animal in the cage with me, I met its gaze, staring it down like I would any other potential threat.

Thank you for my freedom. How may I serve you, Alpha?

The sound of another wolf's voice in my head was something I would have to get used to, but it helped that this wolf did not sound anything like my father's voice. I didn't think I'd have been able to deal with that.

But that was before my mother's scream sounded through the house, ripping my heart in two. I'd taken her mate from her. And as much as it hurt—and it really fucking did—it also gave me hope.

Wren was alive—had to be. Because that ache in my chest was nothing like the pain my mother was feeling.

"Go comfort your mate. Stay with her, protect her, and when I need you, allow me to call on you."

As you wish, Alpha.

I rubbed at the ache in my chest and followed the wolf out of the cell where my father's body moldered. A part of me mourned the man from my childhood. The one who tied my shoelaces and taught me how to fight.

But that man was gone now.

And if anyone else stood in my way of finding Wren, they would be following him into the grave.

TWO YEARS, SIX MONTHS AGO

"Please tell me you're joking."

I leveled my brother with a glare powerful enough to knock the paint off a car, and he snapped his mouth shut. Theo was getting smarter over these last few months, but he should know that I hadn't joked in a long fucking time.

"Six. Months," I growled, my voice as low as I could make it. "I have been hunting for this asshole for six months, Theo. What part of this plan makes you think I'm joking?"

It was bad enough that it had taken this long to find the illusion mage that had taken Wren from me, but it was worse that the Fae that locked all the gods-forsaken

Fae doors seemed to have dropped off the fucking map. After all this time, this was the only lead I had, and I was going to make sure he didn't fall through the cracks.

Again.

But acting now was our only option.

"Maybe because the only protection either of us have is this silly little necklace," he hissed, dangling the charm Fiona made him in front of my face. "Or that the ABI refused to back us up, Mom is against this, and we still can't find Wyatt. Really, the options seem to be endless at this point. Not to mention…"

Theo gestured to the white wolf that hadn't left my side since we'd started this mission. Ghost was a good companion, diligent, and loyal to a fault. The wolf also got under Theo's skin, refusing to heed any command he gave him, tearing up his expensive Italian loafers, and pissing on his seat at the dinner table more times than I could count.

"Oh, get over it," Hannah growled, looking up from her book. It was one of those bodice-rippers from the '80s with the dude with the open shirt and flowing hair. Hannah loved those books, and all it had taken was one single, solitary body slam to teach my brothers not to make fun of her for them. "I've heard you bitch about that damn wolf more than should be allowable by law.

And Fi's charms are top-notch, which you would know if you'd actually shut up for five seconds and listen to anyone else in your family. You're lucky you even got one at all."

That was true. Theo was lucky he got a charm. Considering Fiona had managed to avoid meeting my asshole big brother, making a charm to protect his mind was a little dicey, but she'd done it. Not that Theo would trust anything made for him by a witch, ever, but that was his emotional baggage to deal with and not mine.

"I'm not going to try and convince you again. You're either going with us or you're going home. I won't take your will away, but you aren't fucking with my plan, either." I leveled him with a glare. "So, are you in, or are you out?"

Theo met my glare with one of his own before peeling his gaze away to stare at the cabin nestled in the valley below. It was a small cottage-style home surrounded by trees and a babbling brook for fuck's sake. Smoke bloomed from the chimney, bold as you please, and if neither of us were wearing the amulets Fiona made us, all we'd see is a cove of trees and that damn water.

Theo sighed long and low before nodding his head. "I'm in. If anything, just so you stay breathing long enough to get your woman back."

But the plan was going to work. It would because it had to. I'd spent the last six months telling the ABI to fuck off, turning in my resignation the millisecond the higher-ups refused to look for my wife. I'd never been more disillusioned in my fucking life before the day Erica told me she wasn't allowed to look for Wren.

Or worse?

When she told me that the ABI wouldn't lift a fucking finger to open the Fae portals. We were on our own, and that was that.

That didn't mean that Erica wasn't helping me on the side or that Fiona, Malia, and Hannah weren't playing both sides of the ABI fence. They were. It just wasn't enough.

"Gee, thanks. Your confidence really is inspiring. Now, before I keel over from your outpouring of faith in me, can you get into position?"

Hannah snickered from behind her bodice-ripper while Theo flipped me off. I'd have smacked him in the temple for that, but he sauntered over to his assigned position, adjusting his cufflinks like he was going into a boardroom. Why Theo needed to wear a suit every-where was beyond me. He always said it was because a century ago, that was how everyone dressed, but I called bullshit.

Theo just liked looking important. Or he had a clothing fetish. Dealer's choice.

"You ready, boss?" Hannah murmured, shooting me a look over the top of her book. She and I had come to an agreement these last few months. I wouldn't stop looking for Wren and she wouldn't give me shit about losing my own mate on my watch. I considered it a good enough trade. Plus, she respected me a little bit more since I'd given the ABI the finger and taken over my pack.

That was the thing about ghouls. They appreciated family more than anything, and kin killers were dealt with swiftly, sure, but mates? To harm a ghoul's mate was tantamount to starting a war. It was half the reason the Dumond nest was nearly extinct.

I tipped my chin in a nearly imperceptible nod and Hannah slipped a frilly bookmark in between the pages of her book and stuffed the worn paperback in the back pocket of her jeans.

"You planning on doing anything stupid in there?" she asked under her breath so Theo or anyone else couldn't hear.

My gaze locked on the sweet cabin down the slope. "I plan on doing whatever I have to. If you've got a problem with that, you can stay here. But if you go down there with us, your badge better not be an issue."

Hannah's chuckle was damn near silent as she shook her head. "There's a reason Fiona and Malia stayed behind, and I didn't. I don't have a problem getting my hands dirty."

That was good to know. Because I was getting the information I needed.

One way or another.

Mom was against this course of action, but, then again, she had an inkling of just how unstable I'd been over the last few months. She knew what I was capable of. Losing her mate had made her all too knowledgeable on that front.

So she elected to stay home with Fiona and Malia, protecting them as a good mother would just in case we were unsuccessful. The blowback on what we were about to do could be catastrophic, to be sure. But my brothers and sisters had chosen to come with me.

There had been a lot of changes since I'd taken my father's seat. One, I didn't make anyone do anything. And two? I asked my pack what they wanted to do, making a better environment for everyone.

In theory.

Taking a deep breath, I connected with my pack, giving them the signal to move down the hill to the cabin. Ghost and Hannah moved with me, melting into the shadows as we traversed the steep decline to the tiny cottage.

The scent of cooked meat and spices tumbled from the chimney as peals of laughter reached my ears. Irrationally, rage hit me at their joy. The mage was happy. He had ripped everything good from my life and he was just... happy. Content. Enjoying life to the fullest.

Yes, he had lost his daughter. I understood doing what one had to, to get someone they loved back, but...

My feet picked up speed as I raced for the home. I didn't bother to follow the fucking plan I'd put into place and decided at the last second to kick that door to smithereens just like he'd done to my life. The mage I'd seen in Wren's mind shot to his feet, his hands glowing with a power that wouldn't work on me one bit.

Peter Lewis was about five centuries my senior, but being as old as he was, he wasn't very smart. Peter thought I would go for him directly. Maybe the old me would go for him head-on, but the new me—the one he created—preferred the approach that would get his attention. Dodging a ball of magic, my claws found his daughter's throat before he could get another shot off.

As soon as I touched her, everything seemed to slow, her magic trying to find a way around Fiona's charm. She frowned, her whole body still as a statue, the magic rising on the air as she shoved her power into me. But Fi's spell held true.

"Sorry, sweetheart. We came prepared."

Agent Penelope Lewis hadn't aged much in the twenty-five years she'd been lost to the Fae realm. With her bright-hazel eyes and smooth skin, she didn't look a day over twenty, which was the age she'd taken her ABI identification photo.

But there was a hardness to her eyes, a calculated shell, and that made this so much worse.

"Get your hands *off* her," Peter snarled, fighting against Hannah and Theo's hold as I tightened my fingers around Penelope's throat.

I could sense my pack surrounding the cabin, waiting on standby just in case this turned sideways. Ghost didn't wait with them. No, against orders, he circled the tableau like he was waiting for something.

Ignoring the mage, I asked his daughter, "Do you know who I am?"

Grinding her teeth, she remained silent, a malice to her gaze that told me she was used to not saying a word. Luckily, it wasn't her I needed to talk.

"That's okay. I don't actually need information from you. I do, however, need information from your father. And your pops? He loves you a whole bunch. Why else would he sacrifice my wife to a filthy fucking Fae to get you back?"

Studying her, I wondered what the Fae saw when he picked women to steal. Was it the hair, the eyes? Or was it something else? A power he wished to have, an ability? Or was he just a collector of pretty women as if they were dolls to use at his disposal.

If I got her back, would she have this same hardness to her? Was she even alive? Was she safe?

Wren. My wolf practically howled her name, rattling my skull.

My nose burned, my chest ached, and I fought off the urge to dig my claws into Lewis' neck and rip it wide.

"See, judging by your leg, you're used to torture. But you know what? Your pops isn't used to seeing it."

Lewis blinked, her gaze finding her father's as her cheeks lost their color. She finally understood exactly why we were here.

"Now, I don't want to hurt you, but to get my wife back, I will. I'd do just about anything. All I need is a little information. Your dad coughs it up, we'll leave. No muss, no fuss. Everybody lives. But if he doesn't? I'll rip you apart inch by fucking inch while he watches until he gives me what I need."

It went against everything I was as a wolf—everything I was as a man—to even threaten something like this. Hell, I wasn't sure who I even was anymore with Wren gone. I didn't recognize the man who would threaten this damaged woman. But I also knew I'd do whatever it was I had to get my wife back.

Peter struggled against Hannah's hold, irrationally thinking the ghoul was the one to test. Just to prove him wrong, Hannah snapped his wrist, the bone crunching with barely a flick of her fingers.

"What do you want?" he howled, cradling his hand to his chest as Theo held him up so he faced his daughter.

"A name. Nothing more, nothing less. I need the name of the Fae you dealt with to get your daughter back. You give me his name, and I'll leave."

Lewis' lids closed like I was asking for a billion dollars or a piece of the moon or something. Maybe I was, but this was something they could give me. They just needed the right motivation.

"I-I can't give you that." Peter tried and failed to get out of Theo's hold, the poor bastard cutting himself on Theo's claws as he writhed.

Oh, but he could. He could and he would. Or else.

Meeting Lewis' eyes, I grabbed the hand that had closed around my wrist. "Take a deep breath."

Her lids widened right before I snapped the bone of

her pinky finger, the sick crunch of the bone breaking nearly making me vomit. But she didn't so much as whimper. In fact, other than a sharp intake of breath, Lewis didn't so much as flinch.

Wren.

She had walked right out of the Fae realm, knowing Wren would have the same fate as her. *She knew.*

"Leave her alone. You want me. Torture me." But Peter was wrong. I didn't want to do any of this. I did, however, want that name.

"I need the name, Peter. Give it to me, and I'll leave her alone. Even send a healer your way to fix her hand and her foot. You won't have to run from me anymore. No looking over your shoulder. Give me the name and we'll be square."

That was a lie. We'd never be square after what he'd done, but I wouldn't hunt him until the ends of the earth, either.

"He'll kill us. Don't you get that? If I give you his name, we're dead." Peter thrashed some more, failing at an epic level to learn his lesson.

"You fucking idiot," Theo growled in his face. "What do you think we'll do to you if you don't? You'll watch your daughter die screaming, you prick. Hell, you'll beg for death before I'm done with you. You fucked with a wolf's mate. You should have hidden better."

Illusion mages were known for their control. It was hard to break them because they were so used to keeping calm, staying rational, keeping their illusions going so they didn't miss a beat. Breaking Lewis—father or daughter—wasn't going to be easy, but Theo wasn't wrong.

Honor didn't matter. Wren did.

"You left my wife to the same hell you lived through. To the same people who took your foot, who hurt you over and over. You think I don't know what you lived through? You think that was a secret? Saving yourself only goes so far. You damned another woman, and that makes you no better than scum in my book."

Lewis swallowed hard as she studied my face. She knew. She knew I wouldn't stop until I got what I wanted.

"T-tell them," she whispered, a single tear tracking down her cheek.

Peter struggled again in vain. "No. He'll kill you. Tr —" He cut himself off, nearly spilling the name I needed so desperately.

Okay, change of tactics.

"Take his eye, Theo," I ordered, a thread of command in my voice as I watched Lewis' expression.

Theo let out a dark chuckle. "You have a preference for which one?"

"Nope. You pick."

Peter's scream was piercing, but it had the desired effect.

"I'll tell you," Lewis pleaded, scratching at my wrist with her blunted nails. "Don't hurt him, I'll tell you. His name is Tristan."

My fingers squeezed her throat as I shook her. "His full name. Now."

"Sh-shadowfall. Tristan Shadowfall," she croaked, breath barely passing the hold I had on her airway. "Crown Prince of the Dark Court."

Tricky. But she was leaving something out. "And what name did he use to bind your father in his deal? Because you and I both know I'm not leaving until I have *that* name."

Peter sniffed, swallowed, and whispered a name— the exact name I'd been waiting for. "Drystan. Drystan Haldrir Shadowfall. That is his given name."

Nodding, I pressed the comm button at my ear. Somehow, some way, Fiona had managed to stay quiet through infil and positioning. Hell, she'd probably put herself on mute.

"You get that, Fi?"

Her thick Southern drawl clanged down the line. "Sure did. Testing it now."

There was a slight pause and then a giddy *"whoop"*

of excitement. "Good to go, hoss. It's going to take me some time to find him, but that name lit up like a damn firecracker."

At least one fucking thing went right today. "Good to know. Appreciate the assist."

Fiona huffed. "Like I wouldn't happily chop off my left chesticle for our girl. You going to rip those two assholes apart now? If so, I wanna hop off the call. Plausible deniability and all."

If ever there was a person who knew about plausible deniability, it was the daughter of the Jacobs Coven ringleader.

"I'm still thinking about it."

Fiona *tsked*, her judgment heavy. "Think faster. I'm gonna skedaddle regardless. The squelch of blood hitting the floor turns my stomach."

Then she clicked off the line, knowing the truth of it even before I did. Because right as she hung up, Ghost went apeshit.

The bark that came out of that wolf damn near made the hairs on the back of my neck stand on end. He threw himself at the wall, the wood breaking away to reveal a false panel. Then came the howl, a howl that broke into my brain, wrenching my gut.

"No," Penelope screamed. "You can't go in there. That has nothing to do with you."

When I absorbed my father's power, the whole of the Acosta pack made a home inside my brain. Unlike with Wren, I didn't feel their heartbeats or their emotions, but there was a link that gave me a certain bit of knowledge, a connection in cases of danger and the like.

But one packmate had been lost to me. It hadn't just been six months without Wren. I'd also missed someone who I considered a brother.

And as soon as Ghost broke down that door, I suddenly knew where Wyatt had been since before my wife had been taken from me.

"Sit still. Dayana, get in here and hold this bitch," I snarled, gladly handing Lewis off to my sister as soon as she came in the door. Penelope fought against her hold, but she was weak and tired, and my sister was ready to rip her apart.

"Santi, Frankie, help me." The order came without a choice attached—not that they'd need it. Wyatt's scent reached my nose as my brothers and I ripped the rest of the façade away.

I ducked through the opening, coughing at the stench of six months' worth of unwashed wolf, human waste, and who knew what else. Chained upright to a wall, Wyatt hung from a set of manacles, his body damn near skeletal. His long blond hair was plastered to his face, his body barely moving from his labored breathing.

But as soon as I touched him, he woke, his eyes wide as he flinched away from me.

"It's okay, brother," I whispered, threading all the calm I so did not feel into the pack bond. "We're getting you out of here. Promise."

"Ni-Nico?" Wyatt croaked, his eyes barely focusing on me as he shivered.

"Yeah, buddy. I gotcha. We're bringing you home, okay?"

Hesitantly, Wyatt nodded, and I yanked at the bonds, pulling the metal clear free of the stone walls as I caught my best friend. Frankie took his legs, helping me haul him out of that dank hovel and into the light while Santi stood there vibrating, trying not to lose his fucking mind.

Five minutes ago, Peter and Penelope Lewis would have walked out of this cabin.

Five minutes ago, I had every intention of letting them live.

But that was then, and this was now.

"Take him," I ordered, snapping Santi out of it as I passed Wyatt to my older brother.

I met Peter's eyes. He already knew that he wasn't

making it out of here, and that was just as well. But I'd make him hurt first.

"Has nothing to do with me, huh? That is my pack-mate, my best friend, but you knew that already. What? Did you need him to make the illusion better? Is that it?"

"Sick fucks," Theo snarled, digging his claws into Peter's neck. "You get some kick out of hurting us? What the fuck?"

But I ignored my brother. I ignored everything but how I could possibly hurt this man as much as he had hurt me. The answer was easy enough. He had taken from me to get his daughter back. Now I would take it all from him.

"Peter Lewis, for your crimes against the Acosta pack, you will pay in pain and blood."

He nodded like all of it was expected, only becoming alarmed when I didn't walk straight to him but to Penelope instead.

"You took my heart from me," I whispered just loud enough for the both of them to hear. "Now I take yours from you."

Then my claws tore into Penelope's chest, ripping her heart out while her father watched. I let the organ fall from my fingers like the trash it was.

Peter screamed in agony, fighting against Hannah

and Theo as the pair of them stared at me like I'd just done the unthinkable.

"I'll kill you," he railed. "You're dead, you piece of shit. You just don't know it yet."

Big talk from a man who couldn't wriggle his way out of a paper bag.

Tilting my head to the side, I had to study the mage who had upended my life. "Your death will not be so kind. You imprisoned my friend, you stole my wife, you conspired with a Fae to take from me—from us."

My gaze fell to the white wolf who was vibrating with the same rage that was thrumming from my every pore. "Ghost?"

Yes, my Alpha?

"Lunch."

Ghost's lips went wide, showing every single sharp canine in his large head. And when he was done, Peter was in ribbons and Ghost's fur was the red of freshly spilt blood.

And while I felt every eye in that cabin and the thrum of my pack's unease at my brutality, I just couldn't make myself give a fuck.

This was war.

And war was bloody.

CHAPTER 4

NICO

FOUR MONTHS AGO

Sleep was for the weak.

That was exactly what I told myself as I poured the last drops of the carafe into my mug, contemplating adding a little bourbon to it. But I knew the alcohol wouldn't do anything to help me sleep, just like it wouldn't numb the pain in my chest. That theory had been tested and discarded long ago. Even the thought of going to bed made me want to come out of my skin.

It didn't matter how comfortable the mattress was or if the room was the right temperature. It didn't matter if I was in wolf form or on two feet. None of it mattered.

I hadn't slept right in years, not since...

Rubbing at the ache that had made a permanent home in my chest, I gritted my teeth against the sting. Simply thinking her name wrenched at my heart. It had gotten to the point that I snapped at anyone who said it—anytime I happened to see a redhead on the street, anytime I spoke to Ellie or Alice, or even so much as heard the whisper of the Bannister family.

Holding my shit together just wasn't going to happen. Which was why just the mere hint of a thought about her had me launching the cup—coffee and all—against the wall, splattering the hardwood floor and wall with the very thing that would keep the dreams of her at bay.

That was the real reason sleep evaded me—or rather, *I* evaded *it*.

As much as I tried to keep her out of my conscious thought, she invaded my dreams. Her smile, her laugh, her moans in my ear. The way she never stopped moving, never stopped thinking, never quit trying to be better. She was always reading or cooking or trying something new. And on the really hard nights, memories of the end would come—the ones of her pleading for me to come with her, to help, to not let her get taken. The ones where she screamed my name as she was ripped away from me.

The ones where my dreams turned to nightmares. Ones of her being tortured. Of her being hurt. Of her being killed. Would our bond know if she'd died? Would it know if she... if she... Those were the nights I'd wake up calling out for her. But she wouldn't come back to me. Couldn't. All because of the fucked-up Fae that was currently residing in my basement.

Letting out a primal growl, I swept the papers from my desk. With them, the glass paperweight flew, embedding into the wall. The lamp tipped on its side, the bulb breaking and winking out.

Ghost popped his head up from the floor, his whine letting me know he could feel the turmoil doing my head in. That, and he didn't want to get caught in the crossfire.

Procuring Tristan—or rather, Drystan Haldrir Shadowfall, Crown Prince of the Dark Court hadn't been easy. It had taken Fiona months of storing her power, the right conditions, and a whole lot of help to even summon the bastard. And while she'd been preparing, I'd had the dungeon retrofitted to become the ultimate Fae cage. Because if the Lewis' taught me anything, it was that a good enough cage was all you really needed.

Well, that, and knowing where their weak spots were.

The problem with Tristan? As far as I knew, he

didn't *have* any weak spots. No family, no friends, no allies, no nothing. There was no leverage to be had, and that had pissed me off for about a year now.

Another problem? Tristan did not react to torture. Not waterboarding, or burning, or removing limbs. Not that it mattered—the fuckers grew back almost instantly. Not a damn thing worked on him, and no matter what we did, he just. Wouldn't. Break.

He wouldn't break, he wouldn't talk, and he wouldn't so much as flinch. Not from isolation or starvation or any of the other thousand things we'd tried.

I'd lost hope a long time ago. Because hope? It was for suckers.

I wouldn't ever be getting her back. I wouldn't be opening those gates, and I wouldn't ever be happy again.

I'd thought about just killing him more times than I could count, but a part of me just couldn't do it. It was the "what ifs" that were killing me.

What if he changed his mind?

What if there was another way?

What if she found her way back to me?

With that tiny, infinitesimal grain of hope, I would always be looking, trying, praying that she made it home.

Somehow, I found myself in the basement

dungeon, staring at my prisoner, my chest heaving, my heart racing. In the year Tristan had been in captivity, I had been in charge of his questioning, and while I was desperate, there were a few lines I would not cross.

But today it seemed my humanity, my compassion, my sense of right and wrong was long fucking gone. How I'd managed to hold onto it this long was a mystery.

"Come to play, Alpha? It's been weeks. I thought you'd forgotten about me."

How could I forget about this asshole? He was the key to everything.

The Fae tilted his head to the side, a winsome smile stretching his lips as his wrists hung from the manacles. "You seem to be a might bit worked up, though. I suppose that means I'm in for it, huh? Come on then. Do your worst."

But I had never done my worst. I had never shorn his hair, cut his ears. I had never plucked out his eyes or made him count grains of sand. I had never pumped the air with oxidized iron or cut his Achilles tendon with iron sheers. I never made wounds that would never, ever heal.

I had been kind.

Too kind.

Well, if drownings and burnings and amputations were considered kind. But I hadn't let Theo tear him apart or ask Ghost to eat him for lunch. I hadn't tried my hardest.

That ended today.

"My worst?"

Could I do my worst and stay sane?

Could I break him without breaking myself?

Did it matter?

Tristan's smile trembled a little before beaming wider. "That's what I asked for, wasn't it?"

"Indeed."

Did it matter that I would be broken if it meant she could come home?

Did it matter if it meant she would be in my arms?

No. I would take breaking myself over another day without her.

Slowly, I strode over to the cabinet and pulled out a set of iron sheers. They seemed ancient, the blackened metal heavy in my hand, but I knew they'd been forged with biting spells and the purest metals only a year ago.

Returning to the cell door, I met Tristan's gaze. "Tell me how to open the gates and I won't do this."

His eyes fell to the sheers, his body tightening bit by bit. "What fun would that be?"

Sniffing, I nodded, swallowing down the last of my reservations. A year. He'd been laughing at us for a fucking year. Faster than a striking snake, I slashed, raking the metal across his cheek.

With the silver blades, he hadn't so much as flinched. But with the iron? Tristan hissed as his whole body jolted, the sizzle of his flesh music to my fucking ears.

"You Fae like deals, right?" I ran the tip of the iron blade slowly down his other cheek, relishing every flinch, every howl of agony, every single bubble and pop of his burning flesh. "You open those gates, and I'll let you keep the skin you have left."

The Fae yanked at his bonds—something he hadn't done in the year he'd been down here—pure hate pouring from his eyes. But once he'd composed himself, the bastard was nothing but smiles and attitude.

"Someone woke up on the wrong side of the bed this morning. Finally decided to get serious, then? I was wondering when you'd gather the bollocks to really—"

The iron knife made a home against the vulnerable skin of his neck, the flat of the blade making his flesh sizzle.

"Open the fucking gates. Open one gate. Just give me back my wife."

The fucker had the gall to smile, his filthy, bloody

face breaking into a wide grin. "No, I don't think I will. I fear my father and your wife far more than I fear you." He straightened, sitting up to take the next hit. "So do what you will, wolf. I will not break for you."

Oh, he'd break. The question was whether or not he'd live long enough to give me what I needed.

"So be it."

I trekked back to the cabinet and selected two sets of iron knuckles. This was going to be bloody. Bloody and brutal, and oh, so satisfying.

But... it *wasn't.*

It didn't matter how bloody the Fae's face was or how many times he yelped in pain. It didn't matter how I hit him. There was just no satisfaction to be had. He was hurt, but he wasn't suffering. He would eventually heal from his injuries and then what?

We would be exactly where we were.

All he had to do was be patient, and the Fae were nothing if not patient.

No, he needed something permanent. Something lasting.

Breathing heavy, I flung the iron knuckles off my hands and went back to the cabinet for the sheers. It was said that the Fae were revered by their hair. The longer it was, the more respect they had. It was also said that forcefully cutting a Fae's hair was tantamount to lopping off their balls.

As a child, I'd thought the act was barbaric. Who would hurt another being that way? But now I knew. Now I knew what this particular Fae was capable of—knew just what I would do to break him.

His hair in my fist, I sawed through the bundle with the iron sheers, cutting close enough to his scalp to draw blood, ignoring his feeble protests and weak, struggling jerks to get from my hold.

"Do my worst, huh?" I rumbled, cutting away every scrap of black hair. Even a year in this damn dungeon, it was still straight as an arrow, not a single tangle, and I relished the softness of it as it fell to the ground, mingling with the dirt and filth and blood.

But the Fae wasn't laughing anymore.

Gurgling breaths wheezed through his lungs as he hung listlessly from his bonds. So much like Wyatt had in the mage's cellar that it physically hurt to look at this man. Wyatt had recovered, but he wasn't the man he'd been before his captivity. Or maybe it was just me who had changed.

"Open the gate to my wife," I ordered, the Alpha power in my voice enough to break just about everyone. "Give her back to me, and this ends."

Slowly, the Fae's head rose, and he speared me with

an expression so without hope it rang like a bell in my chest.

"If I have to die here alone and broken to see my family safe, there is nothing you can do to me to make me break. No crimes you could commit, no torture." His smile was despondently blank, the life, the spark that was once there, gone. "There is nothing, wolf."

And his blankness, his sadness made me rage. He was winning. And giving up meant he'd never give her back to me, never let me see her again, never...

My hand rose of its own accord.

"Stop," Mari screamed, racing down the basement steps and throwing herself against the bars. "This isn't you, Nico. Don't let him take you away from us."

But he had, hadn't he? Hadn't he taken away everything that I was? Hadn't he ripped everything good from me? Hadn't he stolen all that I was and all that I would be?

Hadn't he killed me already?

"Put the sheers down, brother. *Please*."

Shaking my head, my fingers tightened around them. "He won't relent, Mari. He won't..."

"I know," she cooed, carefully opening the cell door and putting herself in between us. Trembling, she pulled the scissors from my bloody hand. "But Fiona found a way around him. Just... don't kill him."

But Fiona had been struggling for months to try and work something. She'd tried everything.

"You're lying. You just want me to have hope, but I can't have hope anymore. I can't do it."

Mari's gaze softened as she wrapped her arms around my middle. "She's found a way, big brother. We just need the Fae alive to do it."

Mari began pushing me toward the cell door, walking us both backward as she continued the hug. Could I have stopped her? Absolutely. But I needed this tiny sliver of hope more than I needed air.

"Please tell me that asshole is still breathing. I doubt I could do a damn thing with his ashes," Fiona called from the top of the steps.

Mari pulled back and shut the cell door, positioning herself in front of it like she was guarding the damn thing from me. "He is, thankfully. You really think you can pull this off?"

Fiona trudged down to our level, her thin frame so painfully gaunt it hurt my chest. She'd been struggling just as much as I had. Not sleeping, looking for something—anything—that would bring...

The poor girl would blow over with a stiff wind if she wasn't careful, but what she lacked in body mass, she made up for in power.

"Oh, yeah," Fiona practically growled, her teeth

showing as she eyed the Fae in the cage. "That gate is going to open, dammit. I don't care if I have to use your fucking entrails to do it."

Tristan coughed out a weak chuckle. "You overestimate yourself, witch."

"Fuck you, Pixie Dust," she snarled, damn near throwing herself against the bars. "You're just mad because your last bargaining chip is gone. I don't need you to open anything. Not anymore."

That hope? It grew in my chest, a stoked fire that could go out at any minute.

"What do you need?"

CHATHAM SQUARE WAS A SMALL PATCH OF GREEN IN THE middle of the city. So close to our old apartment, it hurt to be back at the place I'd lost her. The magic in this place was dead, the Fae portals stealing all of it when they closed, but someone, somewhere had been tending to the flowers. And that—as stupid as it was—gave me the confidence that this was going to work.

Fiona had needed an inordinate amount of shit to get this ball rolling. Specifically, she needed the door to the cabin where we'd sealed the mate bond. That was a big enough ask—especially since I wasn't an agent anymore—but then she gave me the rest of the list.

She needed my blood, the Fae's blood, and *her* blood.

The only place I could think of that had her blood on this plane of existence was my father's former office. It was either that or gut Margot Bannister and pray that was good enough. Personally, gutting Margot was still on the table even if the only purpose was to make me smile.

The laundry list of herbs and magical artifacts and salt—holy mother of the gods, the salt—was almost never-ending, but we'd gotten everything Fiona needed. What we didn't get her, was more witches.

The witch community of Savannah had dwindled significantly over the last year. Witches weren't disappearing exactly, just packing up and leaving without so much as a word. Covens with centuries of ancestral magic built up in the dozens of cemeteries, just skipping town. The rats were deserting a sinking ship, and I couldn't blame them. The place I called home wasn't what it used to be with all the Fae doors closed.

It was as if Savannah itself was mourning *her* loss right alongside me.

"Okay, we need to wait until the moon hits its peak,

and then I can start," Fiona mumbled, staring at her watch as she fiddled with an iron blade.

Said iron blade was coated in... *Wren's* blood, the old, dried carpet of my father's study providing what we needed with a little bit of magic.

Wren.

Just thinking her name was a punch to the gut. But if we could get the door open, if we could just do something, it wouldn't feel like I'd lost her.

It wouldn't feel like she was gone forever.

It wouldn't feel like she was... *dead.*

Fiona approached with the knife coated in my wife's blood. "It's time. You ready?"

Holding out my forearm in answer, I nodded, more than ready to get this show on the road. Two years, eight months, four days, six hours, and twelve minutes. That's how long those doors had been closed. It had felt like decades.

Centuries.

Eons.

Fiona sliced through my arm, mingling my blood with Wren's. Then she moved to Tristan, not bothering to give him the same care. She brutally brought the blade down, nearly taking his whole hand with it. The Fae howled in agony, but Fiona paid him no mind. Instead, she positioned herself in the middle of her circle, the chants coming from her lips guttural and lilting all at the same time.

She was speaking Tristan's native tongue. Where she'd learned it, I wasn't sure, but she spoke with the fluid grace of someone who had studied the language for years. And with the blood and the chants and the ingredients, the world as a whole shook, the magic from Fiona spilling out into the night.

A door seemed to spring up from the ground, its edges framed in dark thorns with sharps spikes. A curl of blackened vines topped it, at their center a grim skull with glowing rubies for eyes. Fire kindled at its base, the embers catching on the grass, blackening it at the base.

This was wrong. Wren wouldn't come out of that door. No. No, I wanted the one from before. The one with flowers and green vines and no thorns.

I opened my mouth to say as much when an amber light lit the door as it opened. At the glimpse of red hair, my heart leapt, but I quickly realized that the person walking through wasn't Wren.

Not unless my wife had transformed into a tall, horned, bronze-skinned redheaded man in the last two years. Gold eyes scanned the square as the fire caught the grass, jumping from blade to blade, the iridescent scales on his bare arms shining in the light of the embers.

"You summoned a Prince of Hell by my blood. Where is my kin?" the man rumbled, but he wasn't a man, now, was he? Not if those scales and horns and title were anything to go by.

We'd wanted Wren, but we'd gotten a demon instead.

Fuck.

PRESENT DAY

"What the fuck do you mean you don't know where Nico is?"

Exasperated, I stared at my best friend in the entire world like she had two heads. Was this the last straw in my already-crumbling psyche? Maybe. But I'd walked through a Fae door into what appeared to be a fucking apocalypse after being kidnapped and, and...

It was as if I had stepped right into *Bizarro World*. Savannah was on fire, and people were strolling down the street like nothing was wrong. Like this was normal.

Like an entire city block being ablaze was just a regular Tuesday. Damn near every store was boarded up, there were burning trash barrels in the middle of the streets, and Ellie had just told me I'd been gone for three. Fucking. Years. And that was *after* she aimed a shotgun at my head.

Three years.

Granted, it made a sick sort of sense. The row house I'd called home for just a scant bit of time had been empty, barren, dust covering every surface. Dried blood had stained the hardwoods black, and I didn't know whose it was. I didn't know if my friends were even alive. And Ellie's house was fortified like she was prepping for a zombie apocalypse to descend on Savannah any second now.

But not knowing where my husband was, *was* the absolute last straw. I swear if she told me one more crazy thing, I would pass right on out. Maybe then I'd wake up in a place that wasn't on fucking fire.

Ellie's dark eyes softened with a little bit of pity, her grip getting tighter on my shoulder as she held me up. Why didn't she know where Nico was? How had everything gotten so fucked up? My chest wanted to cave in, and with the worry making a home for itself in my gut, I felt closer to Swiss cheese than an actual person.

"You were gone for so long, Nico couldn't even look at me without—" She shook her head, her throat sounding like she had a frog in it.

Meaning she'd seen him after Tristan had shoved him back with his power. He was alive—or at least he had been.

Three years.

I couldn't imagine losing Nico for three years. I'd been ripped away from him for a day—*tops*—and I was half out of my mind. Three years? I'd be a puddle on the floor.

Ellie stared at the front porch of the house she shared with her mother, tears pooling in her eyes. It was a small home, but once upon a time it was filled with laughter and love and so much warmth. Now it looked like it had seen better days. Three years of shit would do that to a house, I guessed.

And to a person.

"I couldn't look at him either. He'd come around every once in a while, making sure we were safe, but he's the Acosta Alpha now. Not that it means much nowadays."

Acosta Alpha? Did something happen to his dad? And why wouldn't that mean much? The Acostas were practically the kings of Savannah. How could three measly years change three hundred years' worth of power dynamics?

Nothing was making sense anymore.

Nothing.

"I'm so sorry, El," I murmured, latching onto her just as tight as she was to me. Maybe if I hugged her tight enough, she'd know just how glad I was to be back—even if being back meant the whole city was on fire. She was alive, Nico was alive. "Is Alice okay?"

Ellie gave me a wet sort of chuckle. "Of course. She's practically running the hospital. It's about the only place that's still running if you know what I mean. Hasn't gotten so much as a cold since you saved her."

I practically wilted to the pavement. Alice Whitlock needed to stay alive forever and a day if possible.

"We'd better get inside," she croaked, pulling out of reach. "It isn't safe being out too long anymore." Ellie gripped my wrist, dragging me closer to the front door.

But I didn't want to go inside. I didn't want to do anything but find Nico and Fiona and Malia and Hannah. I especially didn't want to be told to calm down and not to worry and to sip some tea.

I wanted answers—answers Ellie didn't seem to want to give me.

Plus, getting dragged places was how this mess got started in the first fucking place.

"Stop," I barked, ripping my arm out of her grip. If it wasn't arcane weirdos or Fae Kings or absolutely incomprehensible Seelie Queens, it was my best fucking friend.

But I didn't want to be touched by anyone, maybe ever again. Not without knowing all the facts about what I'd missed.

"I'm not going anywhere until someone somewhere tells me why Savannah is on fire and why shops are boarded up all over town and why—"

"Well, well, well," a male voice called, sending a bucket of ice water through my veins. It wasn't that his voice was particularly scary or mean. It was that he sounded just like the sinister Fae King that started this whole mess.

I half-expected Desmond to come walking out of the shadows when my gaze left Ellie. Instead, it found one of four Fae men slithering from the murky darkness. Okay, so they weren't slithering exactly, but the way they moved was... wrong. Just *wrong*. I'd never seen a Fae move like that.

With shorn hair and ears, covered in filth and rags and a fair amount of blood, they were unlike any other Fae I'd ever encountered outside of the Unseelie realm. Because the Unseelie realm had their kind in cages.

Beaten and bloody, they appeared half-starved and crazed and...

Feral, my brain supplied, and the old noodle was one hundred percent right. Feral was the best word to describe them.

"You smell of the Dark Court," the talker growled, an expression of hunger on his face as his purple eyes lit with his magic. "Fresh, too. You smell of home. Tell me, witch, how do you smell of our homeland? Tell us which gate you have opened." His smile was predatory, his canines filed to points. "Tell us and I may let you both live."

If his home was the Dark Court and they wanted to go back, these weren't the Fae to fuck around with. These were the Fae to run screaming down the street to get away from.

Awesome. Just what I wanted after my dramatic exit of the Dark Court only to be dragged back to it. *No, thank you.*

"Get in the house, Wren," Ellie hissed, reloading her shotgun and snapping the barrel closed. I could have sworn she'd set it down, but somehow it was back in her hands, and she was ready to fire.

And honestly? That seemed like the best idea anyone had ever had in the history of ever. Shooting first and asking questions later was absolutely the correct course of action. Unfortunately, I didn't make it three paces before the Fae were on us. Gritty hands yanked Ellie right off her feet, the men moving so fast they were a blur of speed. She managed to get a single shot off before her gun fell from her hands, managing not to go off again as it clattered to the concrete driveway.

One of the Fae staggered back, his middle a grizzly mess from the buckshot. But I was more focused on the hold the others had on my best friend. Heat flashed over my body as her screams ripped through the air. The scent of her fear spiced the air with a cloying perfume that made me want to gag.

I didn't even notice the hands on me—didn't even register them tearing me away from her. What I did notice was one of them striking my best friend across the face. Blood stained Ellie's lips and I moved. The speed Nico had shared with me, the animalistic qualities that I'd garnered in just the short time I'd been mated to him, reared their very welcomed head.

It seemed like years ago when I'd sparred with Nico in the courtyard. In a way, it had been years, but that didn't mean I couldn't use every advantage I had against these fucks. Kicking my legs out, I twisted in their grip, tossing one away as I nailed the other right in the gut. But the one that touched Ellie had my full attention, a burning sort of fire churning in my belly as the rage settled in.

And then I wasn't the only one that was burning.

I swear, as soon as the mere thought of fire hit my brain, the Fae that was holding Ellie started screaming, his tattered shirt going up in smoke along with his shorn hair. The problem? My hand was also sort of on fire. On instinct, I flailed my fingers trying to extinguish the flames, but instead of them going out, they just spread, falling from my skin like raindrops onto the very dead grass.

What the fuck?

No, really, when in the blue fuck had fire become a problem I needed to deal with? Sure, once upon a time there had been fire issues when people had done spells around me, but not once in the history of ever had I made fire of my own outside of flicking a fucking lighter.

Ellie wrenched herself out of the burning Fae's hold while I proceeded to catch the grass, one of the other Fae's tattered pants, and my left shoe on fire. Stomping my foot, I managed to get that problem resolved, but the rest...

"You think a little fire is going to stop me from going home?"

The spokesman of the group latched onto my shirt,

dragging me closer as he ignored the growing blaze in my palm. The back of his hand cracked against my cheek, sending a lightning bolt of pain through my whole head. When I could peel my eyes open again, the fire in my palm was out. Sure, his buddy was still writhing on the ground, catching every bit of Ellie's yard on fire, but that wasn't the problem at the moment.

No, the problem was that for the zillionth time in a handful of days—yes, the timeline was debatable—I was being carried somewhere I absolutely did not want to go.

"Get your hands off of her," a man growled, the animalistic cadence to his voice familiar and not, all at the same time.

Rough hands ripped me out of the Fae's grip, and somehow, I was on my feet behind the back of a hulking hooded figure holding a blade. His calloused and scarred hand held me behind him, almost as if he didn't want to let me go.

My heart tripped in my chest. The scent wasn't right, the voice was rougher, harder, but his touch? No one could fake the hold his touch had on my heart.

Nico.

I twisted my wrist out of his grip to put my hand in his and hold it tight. It had only been a day for me and that was too fucking long. It had been years for him.

Years.

But Nico didn't look at me. No, he was focused on the two Fae still standing.

"You're in my way, wolf. Stand aside and I'll let you live."

"You won't touch her again," Nico growled, his voice no smoother now than it was a few seconds ago. "And I remember you barely surviving the last time we did this dance."

"Come to finish what you started, then?" the Fae returned, flicking his shorn ear. The wound was months old, the pointed tip long gone. In stories, Fae would shear their own ears to fit into human society, but I'd never seen it done against a Fae's will.

But Nico didn't answer him.

Instead, he shot forward, taking me with him as he advanced. We moved together as his sword sliced through the air, the bloody squelch of it hitting home sending ice through my veins. By the time Nico stopped moving, the Fae were in pieces on the ground, the bloody limbs twitching as their nerves died. A severed head stared at me, eyes wide in the throes of its death mask.

I fought off the urge to puke.

"What the fuck, Nico?" Ellie griped, resting the stock of her shotgun over her shoulder. "You'd better call one of your brothers to clean this mess up. If Mom sees Fae innards on her front lawn, she's gonna shit a kitten."

Nico flicked blood off his sword before stowing it in the scabbard across his back. Then he gave a sharp whistle. "Ghost. *Lunch.*"

I about jumped out of my skin when a flash of white fur brushed against my hip, the giant wolf seemingly coming from nowhere. The behemoth of an animal made quick work of the Fae—even the charred one— leaving only the stain of blood on the ground.

"I suppose hosing the ground is necessary," Ellie grumbled, stomping off to the side of the house while I stared at the huge white wolf licking his chops, his fur stained red.

Shivering in the heat, I backed up a few steps until the leash of Nico's hold pulled taut.

Then he turned, finally meeting my gaze. His eyes were the same gold color, but that was about all that was familiar. They were harder—hell, his whole face was—with the faint trace of lines fanning out from the corners. A white scar bisected his right eyebrow, and another cut down his cheek toward his mouth. There might have been more, but the rest of his face was covered in a thick beard.

Nico's shoulders seemed to sit wider, his spine straighter. He knocked the hood of his coat off his head, revealing he hadn't cut his hair since I'd been gone, the strands reaching past his shoulders.

All of that came to me in the periphery, my focus on his eyes and how hopeful they seemed. He reached for me, his bloody hand trembling as it nearly made contact with my skin.

"*Wren*," he breathed. "Is it really you?"

CHAPTER 6

Nico

It couldn't be. Could it?

Years of searching—of spells, of all-out war—and she just shows up one day out of the blue? The wolf beneath my skin howled to get free, calling me to this very spot. Calling me to her.

"Nico?"

Just the sound of her sweet voice made my knees weak. My hands found her face, the Fae's blood staining her skin red, but I didn't care.

Wren.

There were so many questions I wanted to ask and none all at the same time. What questions mattered when she was here? There had been a time that I would gladly sell my soul to have her in my arms and here she was.

Healthy and whole.

Alive.

I ducked, pressing our foreheads together as I took her scent into my nose for the first time in three years. Other than the faint trace of Fae, she smelled exactly the same—that same honey and jasmine perfume that was all her.

And all I wanted to do was kiss her and hold her and make sure she never got hurt again.

"Missed you, Bird. Missed you so fucking much."

Then my lips were on hers, the warmth of them making me feel alive for the first time in years. That ache in my chest—the one that had me practically clawing my own heart out of my body? It had eased, my heart picking up speed as I drowned in her, our tongues tangling as I drank her down.

My arms found their way around her waist, clutching her to me with a roughness that scared me a little. My brain was screaming at me to be gentle, but my wolf was doing the exact opposite. He wanted our fangs in her neck and her heat surrounding us and her moans down our throat.

And he was getting harder and harder to ignore.

Lifting Wren off her feet, my palms found the swell of her ass, and the carnal moan that came out of her when the ridge of my erection brushed her center was fucking bliss. And she was wearing the same dress that she'd left me in—the odd dichotomy of frilly floral sundress and combat boots that had made my dick hard three years ago. I'd had plans for that dress, if I remembered right, and those plans were coming true just as soon as—

"Are you two planning on fucking on the front lawn or is finding someplace private on your to-do list? I'm sure the demons running around here would love a good show, but I'm going to need some eye bleach."

I loved Ellie Whitlock like one of my sisters, but now was not the time for her brand of humor.

Wren's lips broke from mine, her wide green-gold eyes lighting up with her magic. "Did she say demons? I could have sworn she said demons."

The sheer amount of shit we needed to discuss was vast, but my dick had other plans for the next twenty-four hours and talking about demons was not on that list. My grip tightened on Wren's ass, before I set her back on her feet and aimed a glare at her best friend.

"I'm taking her home. I'll make sure the boys patrol this area tonight. Make sure the Fae know to stay away."

Ellie rolled her eyes as she sprayed blood off the pavement. "Just let her come up for air sometime in the next week, will you?"

Her gaze shifted to Wren who seemed just as

confused and alarmed at the demon talk as she was a minute ago. "And don't worry about the demons. They keep to themselves. Mostly."

Wren just blinked at her, her mouth agape. "I cannot begin to tell you just how not comforting that statement was."

But Ellie was right. The demons weren't the ones we needed to worry about. Wren peeled out of my grip, enveloping her best friend in a hug so tight it was a wonder Ellie could breathe. "I'm coming back tomorrow. You have to fill me in on all I missed, okay?"

Ellie squeezed her back, but smartly said, "You'll be back sometime next week when he finally lets you up for air. I'll be here when you're ready, babe. Now that you're back, there's no rush."

She was reluctant to let Wren go, but finally managed it with teary eyes and a pinched mouth. Wren was home. She was back. She was safe.

And she is ours.

My wolf had not quit his incessant howling, but he was right on that front.

Wren was ours. And she needed to come home where it was safe.

Without another word, I pulled Wren back, guiding her toward home. The warmth of her hand in mine was everything I'd wished for. In my wildest dreams, she came to me like this—showing up one day out of the blue. A sick part of me wondered if I was still dreaming, if none of this was true.

But my heart and my wolf did not give that first fuck.

Walking in Savannah was a necessary evil. With as many stalled, burned-out cars cluttering the road, there wasn't much use for driving, anyway. Still, it wasn't exactly safe. The demons that followed Zephyr out of the Hell gate were nice enough. The real deterioration to the city came when the Fae topside couldn't use them to go home.

That may have started a mini war between the species that pretty much fucked over the rest of the city. And with the ABI too busy making sure the world stayed none the wiser about our little predicament down here, the war raged on unchecked.

Well, sort of.

How Wren had made it here unscathed made my chest start hurting all over again. Just seeing those Fae with their hands on her made me want to rage. Tucking her under my arm, I guided us west toward home and buried my nose in her hair. Ducking into an alley between two burned-out buildings, we picked our way through trash and rubble.

Do you wish me to scout the way, Alpha? Ghost's voice

rang in my head, yanking my focus back to the matter at hand. We needed to get three miles down the road without incident.

Sure. No problem.

Wren startled under my arm, staring at Ghost's retreating back like he was an actual ghost. "Did that wolf just talk to you. Like in your head?"

That gave me pause. "You heard him?"

No one else in the pack could hear Ghost—not even in their wolf form. Only me.

"Of course I heard him. He burrowed right into my brain and—" She stopped, resting her hands on her knees as she wobbled. "This is too much. Wolves just speaking inside my brain and Savannah is on literal fire and Ellie damn near blew my head off and evidently, it's been three fucking years, but to me it's only been a day, and the Fae could touch me here, but they couldn't touch me there and—"

Some things just never changed.

Cupping her cheeks, I pressed a kiss to her trembling lips, stopping her rant mid-sentence. I had never missed someone freaking out like I'd missed Wren's epic meltdowns. I had never wished to solve a problem or ached to listen to someone like this. Being Alpha I heard a lot about other people's issues, but Wren's was the only ones I wanted to solve.

She's here.

She's alive.

Her scent enveloped me, quelling that ache in my chest once more—the one I never thought would go away.

"Tell me, Bird," I murmured against her lips as I hauled her up into my arms, her legs wrapping around my waist like they were made to do it. "If I fuck you against this wall, will that make it all better, or—"

This time it was me that was cut off, her kiss searing a path all the way down to my dick. It had been so long since I'd had her touch, so long since her scent filled my nose and her softness in my arms. It had been so long since I'd had any sort of bliss—and having Wren's mouth on mine, her body close to mine, her ass in my hands was indeed bliss.

Two steps later, her back was against the rough brick wall and her hands were at my belt. Wren broke our kiss, moving to my jaw, my neck, the rake of her growing fangs at the tender skin sending chills down my spine.

Three years.

Three years without her touch. Without her kisses. Without her teeth at my neck, without her smile. Three years of searching.

Fuck.

I pressed the bulge in my jeans against her center, the heat of her calling my name. My whole body thrummed with her desire, her need, her emotions. I'd missed them so much, even though they nearly made me mindless. It took everything inside of me not to tear the fabric away and just plunge inside her.

Are we really doing this here?

For lack of a better term, this was indeed in public, and it wasn't safe with Fae crawling around, and...

The war raging in my brain died a swift death as her hand closed around my cock.

"Fuck me, Nico," Wren breathed, her voice hitching as my thumb raked across her tight nipple. "I need you."

Yes. We were doing this here and now.

"I fucking need you, too."

Hiking up her skirt, it took less than a second to rip her underwear out of the way and notch the head of my cock against her opening. My eyes practically rolled into the back of my head at her heat searing into me. And then I pushed inside, her gasping breath against my lips everything I wanted and more.

I paused a second, the need warring inside me almost too strong. My wolf was so close to the surface, I could hurt her and not mean to.

Wren's finger found my chin, jerking it so I had to meet her gaze. "I told you to fuck me, Nico." The walls of her pussy fluttered around my cock, nearly undoing me right there and then. "I didn't say be gentle. I didn't say be polite. We'll do polite later. Fuck me like you missed me. Now."

She even used a bit of my Alpha in her voice like she'd been the one who'd been crowned and not me. Fuck, she was so fucking sexy it almost hurt.

"Yes, my queen," I growled as I thrust into her, earning a gasp that quickly morphed into a moan.

I fucked her like a man possessed. I fucked her like I hated her, like I blamed her. Like she was the reason I'd spent the last three years alone. Like she was the guilty one and not me.

Her moans were loud enough to wake the dead, but I couldn't for the life of me silence them—I'd missed them too much. So instead, I swallowed them, kissing her as she whimpered into my mouth, her needy mewls sending fire straight down to my balls.

Fuck.

I was going to unman myself right here in this alley.

Breaking the kiss, I yanked at her dress, exposing one of her luscious breasts to my mouth. Her breath hitched, but she needed more. I didn't wait three fucking years to have our reunion ruined by my overeager dick.

"Open," I ordered, cupping her jaw. She did as told,

and I thrust my thumb into her mouth. She eagerly sucked it, curling her tongue around the tip like she'd once done to my cock. Roughly, I pulled it free, finding her clit with the now-wet digit.

Circling the tight bud, I met her eyes, watching them glow with heat and magic and the wolf she didn't have.

"You're going to come for me, Bird. You hear me? You're going to come right the fuck now."

My thumb circled once, twice, three times and then she was coming apart, a silent scream showing me the flush of her perfect skin, her pleasure, the fangs that I ached to have in my own throat.

Without warning, she struck, burying those sharp teeth into my mating mark like it had a beacon guiding her there. My release slammed into me, pulling me under before I could even take a breath. My fangs ached with it, finding her skin and cutting through it without conscious thought on my part. A second release crashed through her, the bite's effect radiating through our bond.

Damn near boneless, I clutched her to me, relishing the feeling of a satisfied woman in my arms as the breaths heaved in my chest. When both hers and mine slowed, I gently helped her get her clothes to rights. Her underwear was somehow not in complete tatters, but the strap of her dress was toast.

I slipped the sword off my back and out of my coat, placing it over her shoulders and zipping it all the way up. "Sorry. I didn't mean to—"

Guilt suffused me, twisting my gut until I was ready to beg her forgiveness. Wren deserved more than an alleyway fuck. More than me ripping her clothes. She—

"Stop." Soft hands reached for my face, cupping it like I was the most precious thing she'd ever seen. "Don't think for a second that I didn't love every minute of what we just did. I asked for rough and you gave it to me. Understand?"

Tipping my chin in a truncated nod, she raised a single eyebrow. *Fine.* "I understand, Bird."

"Good. Now, quit feeling like shit because you're harshing my mellow and I think I'm going to need it a lot before we get home." Her gaze panned over the alleyway. "Speaking of home, where is it? Also, I really like this." She reached up and gently pulled at a strand of my hair.

I hadn't cut my hair in three years. Now it was past my shoulders and an epic nuisance. Grumbling, I pulled it into a knot at the back of my head with an elastic band I'd had to steal from one of my sisters.

"Don't get too attached to it."

"Aww, come on," she pleaded, circling my middle in a hug. "Let me have it for just a little while longer? And the beard. I *really* like the beard."

Smiling, I pressed a kiss to her forehead. If she wanted me to be a double for Rapunzel and keep a mountain man beard, I'd do it. I'd do damn near anything. If it meant she was staying here with me, if it meant she was really here, if it meant she was by my side for the rest of my life, I'd do any fucking thing she wanted me to.

"Come on, Bird. I'll show you the way home."

CHAPTER 7

WREN

The harried trek to Nico's home was marginally uneventful. Other than sidestepping a burning car and ducking behind a building to avoid a roving group of listless Fae, the two-mile journey was peaches and fucking roses. I hadn't really taken it all in when I'd raced to find Ellie, but it was so much worse than I'd thought.

By the time we reached the Acosta pack house, the shock of it all had taken its toll. I'd lost three years. And in that time the world had literally gone to shit. Blinking away tears, I stared at a place I thought I'd never see again.

Nico's childhood home had changed significantly from the last time I'd stood in this very driveway. For one? It was shrouded so heavily by overgrown live oaks I barely recognized it, the Spanish moss and branch both going unchecked since I'd seen it last. Two? It was cloaked in enough magic, even I had a hard time looking at the joint. Normally glamours weren't a problem for me, but this was just unreal.

"Come on, Bird. Let's get off the street."

Again, I wanted no part of this home, but for a very different reason this time. Last time I worried they wouldn't like me. This time I was just keen on keeping my head attached to my shoulders and my blood in my veins. But I kept my mouth shut, though, holding tight to Nico's hand as I followed him and Ghost inside.

My gaze immediately went to the closed door of Nico's father's office, and of its own accord, my hand reached for my neck. I wondered if that room was the same. Did they put it back to rights? Or was my blood still staining the carpet, blackened with age?

"Bird?"

Startled, I tore my eyes from the door and found Nico. "Yeah?"

His golden gaze centered on me just a little, making me suck in a breath to my frozen lungs.

"He's gone, you know. And Diana has been banished for years. And my brothers will never touch you again. I swear it. I know you think—" He shook his head, pulling me closer. "I actually don't know what you think, but there is so much to tell you, so much."

I probably should have felt relieved, but I didn't. There were demons walking the streets of Savannah, and somehow, something told me that I was the cause. There was no way I wasn't going to get blamed for that. There was no way that Diana wasn't right about me.

What had Áine said? That I was breaking the Fae realm? What if I did that here, too? Was anyone safe around me?

"It's fine. I'm fine." That was a total and complete lie. Three years? Three years. Just gone.

Nico squinted at me, his skepticism palpable. "You know that I can feel you, right? It's how I knew you were back, how I knew to find you. Knew you were in trouble." He tapped his chest over his heart three times. "You live here. Inside me. Your emotions, your heartbeat, the breath in your lungs. I missed it so much when you were gone. It was an ache that never went away. So, I know exactly what you're feeling, and I'm going to make sure you never feel this way again."

He let my hand go and cupped my jaw, pressing his forehead against mine.

"You will be safe and warm and loved, and I don't care if I have to move heaven or hell to do it, either."

The sheer determination on his face would be scary

to anyone else. To me? It was a promise I knew he would die to keep.

And that was the problem.

"Like I said, I'm fine. It's just a lot, you know? I'll adjust."

Pressing a kiss to my lips, he eased some of the dread pooling in my belly, so I supposed that was a start.

"Holy fucking shit," a familiar voice called from the top of the stairs. I practically wilted in Nico's arms as Hannah and Malia sprinted down the staircase.

Hannah was just as stone-faced and stoic as ever, but she'd changed her hair quite a bit. It was now down to her waist, dyed a midnight-purple color that seemed to shimmer to cobalt in the right light. Malia was slightly less buttoned up, her hair hung loose around her shoulders, the curls only slightly tamed instead of her usual painfully tight bun. And instead of high-collared button-up shirts and wide slacks, she was in cargo pants and a fitted long-sleeve top with a deep scoop neck.

The biggest change? Her hands were free of gloves. And of all people, it was Malia who damn near tackled me in a hug.

"I can't believe it. Holy shit. Oh, my gods." She

pulled away, staring at me like I couldn't be real. "I tried everything. I could never see you. Holy shit."

Tears filled her eyes before I was wrapped in another hug, her ironclad hold one I didn't want to break.

"Quit hogging her," Hannah griped before wrapping us both in her long arms. Being damn near six and a half feet tall, she had no problem squeezing the shit out of us both. "What happened? How did you get back?"

Shrugging, I opened my mouth only to close it again. How could I answer them? They had gone through so much—suffered so much—and for me it had only been a day.

A bad day, sure, but a single day, nonetheless.

"Is this for real?" Someone else said, accompanied by a thunder of several feet.

I was pulled out of Hannah and Malia's hold to get damn near squeezed to death by Nico's little sister Mari. "He told us through the pack bond, but holy shit. I swear half of us thought he was hallucinating or something. Holy fuck buckets, where have you been, girl?"

Someone pulled me from Mari, and I was patted on the back and hugged and squeezed by more people that I could shake a stick at. Lara gave me a one-armed hug with a toddler on her hip and Dayana picked me up right off my feet with happy tears in her eyes. Luckily, I was rescued once the love got overwhelming. Nico pulled me away from everyone with a gentle growl, fitting me under his arm like he'd shank them if they got too close.

"Let's get you some food and—" Nico began before I cut him off with a question that should have been on my lips from the get-go. There was a person missing from this massive huddle and the fact that she hadn't come down those stairs screaming her head off was the real concern here.

"Where's Fiona?"

I met Hannah's gaze as she stared down at me for a second before she turned to Nico. The look on her face said, "Your call, boss" and that was a very, very bad thing. A "no-good, very bad, oh, fuck" kind of a thing.

"She's fine," Nico said, but there was the teensiest bit of a lie there. "She's alive, she's conscious, she's—"

"She's under house arrest," Malia finished for him. "We'll tell you all about it, and you can see her for yourself in a minute. She'll be really happy to see you."

I was still stuck on that last bit. "House arrest?"

What the fuck had Fiona done to earn herself a punishment—especially with everything going on? Nico had filled me in a little on the way here. The ABI was in shambles trying to keep Savannah contained, but the Fae pretty much worldwide were losing their fucking minds. Luckily there weren't a ton of them on this side, so only the densely populated cities like Savannah, New York, New Orleans, and San Francisco were having instability.

Plus, Savannah was the only one with an active open Hell gate, so we were essentially ground zero for the fuckery. The ABI had cordoned off Savannah like it was a CDC black zone, quarantining us to the rest of the world. There was enough magic at the border to keep almost everyone in. Granted, some arcaners were leaving in droves—those with enough money and connections to grease the wheels of bureaucracy and cut through the red tape.

He had missed the part about how the Hell gate opened, though, and what they were doing to close the damn thing.

"I can eat later. I want to see her now."

"I don't think so," Catia said in a mom voice that had my shoulders reaching for my ears. "I can hear your stomach rumbling. When was the last time you ate?"

That was a hard question to answer. "Breakfast the day I left. But time is different there. I think it's only been a day or two for me."

Granted, I was unconscious for a little bit, so that timeline could get pushed a little left, but the truth of the matter was it hadn't nearly been as long for me as it had for them.

"Remind me never to go through a Fae door," Santiago muttered, eyes wide as he stared at me like I had spontaneously grown a second head.

Frankie smacked his little brother on the arm with the back of his hand. "There aren't any open Fae doors to go through, moron."

"One day or three years, doesn't matter." Catia grabbed my hand from Nico's and slung an arm over my shoulder. "You need food. I'm making you a plate and you're going to eat until you can't anymore, you hear me?"

"I'm fi—"

Catia's eyebrow should be against the Geneva Convention and classified as a war crime. "If you finish that word, so help me, I will force feed you until your stomach bursts. Then you can get a shower, and after that, you can go see Fiona. No offense, sweetheart, but you smell like a dungeon, and not a nice one."

I didn't want to tell her that was exactly where I'd been, so I kept my mouth shut, following her lead to the kitchen where far more people sat around the counter, spilling into the dining room. Every single person froze when we walked in—stopping mid-conversation and mid-bite.

Oh, good. Just what I always wanted. An audience to my awkwardness.

"Most of the pack lives here with us on the compound now." Catia grabbed a plate and started loading it down with more food than I could eat in a week. "With so many humans gone, we commandeered the surrounding properties for our use, but more often than not, we eat here. It's good to have a touchstone of family while everything is..." She trailed off, shaking her head as she dumped gravy on the mashed potatoes.

"At least there's many hands and all that. Makes it easier."

I had the hardest time wondering what I was supposed to be doing. Was I supposed to wave? Everyone was staring at me... But then I realized maybe they weren't staring at *me* but *us*. Studying Catia, I noticed the changes in her that I'd missed in all the hubbub. There was a sadness to her, found only in the lines of her shoulders and the tightness to her eyes. She was smiling at me, but I still saw the hurt and fear and pain behind the mask.

I didn't know what had happened to make Nico the Acosta Alpha, but I knew it had to have involved losing Tomás. And as much as he had hurt Nico, as much as he'd hurt me, I'd never wish her to lose her husband over it.

"Come on, sweetheart. I made lemon tarts just for you."

A sting hit my eyes making me blink hard, so I didn't start bawling in the middle of this kitchen surrounded by all these people.

"Thank you," I managed to choke out before a distinct growl made everyone more than freeze.

I looked up to an irritated Nico crowding into me, but his eyes were on his pack.

"Give us a minute, everyone."

Waving away his order, I shook my head. "No, no. I'm fine. Everything is fine. They are enjoying their meal. Let them be."

But my eyes did that stupid thing, like filling to the brim and spilling over, and Nico was having none of it. "Out."

I swear, that kitchen was cleared in two seconds, flat. Nico's whole family just up and left the room, no questions asked—even his mom—which made me feel like the biggest heel on the planet. Heat rose in my cheeks, and I forced myself not to duck my head—not that Nico would let me.

His rough hands cupped my face, making me look at him. "What is it, Bird?"

Sweet mother of the gods, can I not be a basket case for like three seconds?

"You're being overprotective," I grumbled, pulling out of his grip. "It's not a big deal. They were happy tears, anyway."

"You've been doing good so far with everything. It's oka—"

Oh, for fuck's sake.

"Your mom made me lemon tarts," I hissed, dashing away the tears that practically burned my skin. "She remembered that I loved them and didn't get to try one the last time I was here, and she made them just for me." I sniffed, praying a hole would just open up underneath me and swallow me up. "That's why I was upset. It has nothing to do with the pack or my trauma from the Fae realm or anything else. Your mom was kind, and it took me by surprise is all."

Gold lit in his eyes before he reached for me, folding me into a hug so warm and soft and safe, the tears threatened again.

Fuuuuucccck. Get it together, Wren.

"In case you weren't aware, the first chance I get, I'm ripping your mother's heart right out of her chest. That is if that craven bitch even has one."

I let out a watery chuckle. "You mean you haven't killed her yet? *Slacker.*"

"Yeah, well, I was more focused on finding you."

As far as excuses went, that was a good one. "Fine.

I'll let it go just this once. Now can everyone come back and eat their freaking food?"

Nico was the Alpha and here he was married to Crybaby McGee and her merry band of sniffles. I swear, I needed a keeper.

And maybe a lobotomy.

Nico let out a piercing whistle and it was as if the floodgates opened. People streamed back into the kitchen, their conversations spilling through the door and over me in a wave of noise. It was so much better than the record-scratch event of earlier.

But the best was Catia's hand resting in the middle of my back as she put two of those lemon tarts on the edge of my plate.

It took a damn age before I could get downstairs to see Fiona.

If it wasn't Catia's raised eyebrow making sure I ate every morsel on my plate, it was Nico ensuring no one in their right mind even so much as looked at me sideways. Considering what happened after the last dinner we had in this house, I couldn't say I blamed him.

He crowded me at the corner of the kitchen island, offering me a cushy barstool while he stood at my back, his hand never leaving me. If it wasn't threaded with my own, it rested on the small of my back or on my leg. It fiddled with the hem of my dress or played with the ends of my hair. It was as if he was reassuring himself that I was real—that he wasn't dreaming—and that made my heart hurt more than I could possibly say.

I wolfed down my food, my hunger getting the best of me. As soon as the first bite hit my tongue, it was as if I hadn't eaten in a week. Granted, it was totally possible it had been more than a day or two in the Fae realm.

"At least she can eat," someone said under their breath, "even if she is a wi—"

Dayana and Mari both smacked a tall man upside the head, but that didn't stop Nico's growl sounding like a thing straight out of a nightmare as his chest vibrated against my back like my own personal guard dog.

Oh, shit, here we go.

This just wouldn't do. I couldn't have Nico threatening every asshole who called me a name, and Nico's pack hadn't even been introduced to me yet. I put a quelling hand on Nico's arm before hopping off my barstool to go meet the tall wolf who probably had a beef with witches.

The energy coming off of him meant he was probably in the seventy- to hundred-year-old range, and his shoulders were beefy and corded with muscle, meaning he could likely bend me like a pretzel. Plastering a beaming smile on my face, I held out my hand to the guy.

In for a penny and all that.

"Hi, I'm Wren. What's your name?"

The guy frowned at my outstretched hand like no one in the history of ever had offered one to him. They'd probably been too scared he'd crush it.

"Zaid," he rumbled, gently taking my fingers in his and shaking it like he could break me if he didn't concentrate. It was either that or touching me made him want to throw up. You know, dealer's choice.

"Now, I get it, like most of y'all, you probably have a problem with the Bannister family. If you know anything about them, though, you'd know I am the black sheep and hate them probably—if not more—than you do. So in a way, we're on the same side, right?"

Zaid's face solidified like I was speaking in tongues, his jaw twitching as he geared up to be an asshole. "No. A witch can never be on the same side as a wolf." He looked past me to Nico, deciding to fuck up in a spectacular fashion. "They all deserve to d—"

"Enough," I growled, pulling on Nico's Alpha before this asshole said something he couldn't take back. "I have had it up to here with bullshit for one day. I went toe-to-toe with a Fae King and laughed in his fucking face. Do you honestly think I'm scared of you? You think you can *bully* me? You think you can hurt my *feelings*?"

I swear if it wasn't Diana, it was Desmond, or my mother, or fucking Ames. What was it about me that just pulled the assholes out of the woodwork?

"You might not like me, and that's fine. Based off your attitude, we probably won't be besties anytime soon. But you will respect my husband or so help me I will put you in the fucking ground. We clear?"

Zaid's gaze dropped when I didn't so much as flinch.

"I asked if we were clear. Are we?" I gestured to Dayana, Lara, and Mari, and a few of Nico's brothers who looked like they were ready and willing for this shit to pop off, crowding Zaid like they were all too eager to cut out a cancer. "Because if I don't put you in the ground, I have more than enough people at my back to do it for me. That is if your Alpha doesn't rip out your heart and fucking feed it to you."

Nico's warmth at my back was punctuated by a low growl that had heat thrumming through my veins and the hairs on my neck standing on end.

"My queen asked you a question," he rumbled, circling my middle with his arm and hugging me to his front. "Answer her."

Zaid's lips pursed like he had to fucking think about it, and that was right about when I lost it for the day. He wanted to call my bluff? *Fine.*

One second, Zaid was douching it up with his lip-purse, and the next, his big body was embedded in the kitchen drywall, blinking at me like I was a gods-damned wizard or something. Now, I would totally allow that I had surprise on my side. No one expected a five-foot-and-some-change, noodle-armed witch to put a seven-foot behemoth through a wall—not even said seven-foot behemoth.

Hell, especially the behemoth.

They also hadn't expected me to yank him out of the wall by the scruff of his neck, walk him outside, and dump his big ass on the back lawn, either.

Wide, dark eyes stared at me, but that stupid fucking look was off his face.

"You think about apologizing, you can come back inside, and we'll forget this bullshit ever happened. You act like an asshole one more time and I'll make you regret it." Raising a single eyebrow, I asked my question again: "Are we clear now?"

"Crystal, my queen," he croaked, back flat on the ground and hands up like a submissive little puppy.

I didn't know if I liked that whole "queen" business but if it made assholes like Zaid shut up and sit down, I was all for it. If I was a queen, Nico would be their king, and he needed someone watching his back. A part of me wondered if I was good enough to do that job, but it wasn't like I could quit now.

Grumbling, I went back to my plate and my half-eaten mashed potatoes that were conspicuously warm, even though it had been a solid minute since I'd taken a bite. Didn't matter. Food was far more important and filling my belly was at the top of my to-do list.

"Holy shit, Wren. Why again did your husband have me watching your back?" Hannah let out a deep belly laugh when I flipped her off as I kept stuffing my face.

"That was hot as fuck, Bird," Nico whispered in my ear, and I had to fight off a shiver because his voice was doing ridiculously awesome things to my belly.

Ignoring him, I nabbed the first of two lemon tarts and popped it into my mouth. Flavor exploded across my tongue and my eyes rolled up into my head. I was pretty sure I moaned, too.

Before I knew it, I was off the barstool and being dragged by the hand up the stairs.

"Nico? What th—"

Then I was pressed against Nico's incredibly hard front, his golden eyes blazing as his warmth, his desire, his mindless craving filled our bond. It was enough to make my knees weak.

"Three years, Bird." His grip tightened on me, and

the thick bulge in his pants pressed against my belly. "Three years of those moans I missed."

Dammit. I wanted him so much I ached. Ten seconds ago, I was happy to get food in my belly, and now so much lust was pounding through my veins, I was damn near crazed with it.

Pressing up to my tiptoes, I nibbled on his bottom lip, the fangs that seemed to grow with my anger or desire nicking his lip. His eyes flared as a single drop of blood welled from the cut, but they went heavy-lidded when I darted out my tongue to steal the drop.

Then we weren't in the hallway anymore. One second, I was savoring the tangy flavor, and the next, I was over his shoulder with Nico's clawed hand holding my ass in place. Each point of those claws holding but not piercing my flesh made me slick between my legs.

Nico set me down in a large bathroom and flipped on the shower, his shirt gone before I had time to adjust to being vertical again. In the periphery I knew the bathroom was huge, with a ten-person shower and a large soaking tub. There were spa-like features but all I could focus on was him. His smooth golden skin was interrupted by long scars and a few burns. I refused to think about what he'd gone through to get them—what could cut him bad enough that even his wolf couldn't heal him. But damn if they didn't just add to everything that was Nico.

Another moment later and Nico was naked, his thick cock standing up and proud, making my mouth water. And while I would have loved to undress him myself, I couldn't help but enjoy the show as he stalked toward me. Nico's focus was so acute, it was as if I was the only woman on the planet, and that reverence—that almost worship—it was the most potent of drugs.

His hands found the zipper of his jacket and yanked, pulling the heavy fabric off of me. I tried to help him with my dress, but he walked me backward to a wall, putting one of those claws to my lips. Then he ran the sharp blade-like talon down my neck, not cutting, but scratching, the danger there and not, all at the same time. When he got to my dress, he curved his finger—slicing through the fabric *and* my bra, in a single clean stroke.

Softly, he ran it down my belly before cutting through my underwear, too, baring all of me to his hungry gaze. His eyes roved over me like a caress, making me shiver with how visceral it felt. Steam clouded the room, fogging the mirror and the glass shower doors. The thick air made the giant bath seem smaller as it curled around us.

He knelt at my feet and worked the laces of my

boots, removing the last vestiges of clothing as my heart tripped in my chest.

"You're so fucking beautiful, Bird."

Instead of responding, I reached for him, unable to wait for whatever he wanted to do next. I needed his touch on my skin—everywhere—but first...

Grabbing his hand, I dragged him to the shower, shoving him under the spray. Water spilled over his head and shoulders, darkening his hair to black.

Nico was wrong. He was the beautiful one, not me.

"Wha—"

"When was the last time someone took care of you?" I asked, pushing him to the stone bench, and forcing him to sit. "And I don't mean making you food or stuff like that."

While I waited for my answer, I found the shampoo and poured some into my hand. Then I fit myself between his thick thighs. His fingers caressed my skin, circling the top of my legs and pulling me closer.

"No one has ever taken care of me like you do. No one else ever will."

As awful as it was, I was so fucking happy that no one had touched him like this while I was gone.

"It makes me a horrible person that my first thought is 'good,' isn't it?" I massaged the shampoo into his hair and relished the near-silent groan that escaped him at my touch.

"No," he rumbled, his voice damn near a purr. "Because if you were in the same position as me and I was the one gone, I'd be just as happy no one touched you like this but me. Call it selfish or toxic or possessive, I don't give a fuck. But me turning to someone else was never going to be in the cards."

That made me both ridiculously smug and hurt deep in my chest all at the same time. If anyone needed to be taken care of, it was Nico. Working my nails over his scalp, I soaped his long hair, praying all the while that he found comfort.

Well, that, and that he'd never cut it.

Gently, I tipped his head back and rinsed his hair, enjoying the show as the soap raced down his body. His grip on my thighs got tighter, pressing our wet bodies together. His rough beard tickled my breasts before his lips closed around a nipple.

"This isn't about me," I gasped, squeezing my knees together to alleviate the ache in my sex. "I want..."

But I didn't get to finish that sentence before his lips were on mine and he was pulling me onto his lap. His hard cock rubbed against my clit in the most delicious way as I moaned into his mouth. Then his hands were in my hair, massaging my scalp, the scent of his shampoo filling my nose once again.

Not breaking the kiss, I reached for his body wash, pouring it in my hands before slipping it over his skin. It was a "two birds, one stone" kind of a deal. I wanted my hands all over him, and it had the added benefit of getting that awful Fae scent off his skin.

Growling, Nico gently pulled my hair, exposing my neck to his mouth as I rocked against him, my hips moving of their own volition. All it would take was the right twist of my hips and he'd be inside me, filling me so full. He rinsed the shampoo from my hair, running his hands all over me as the soap cascaded down my body.

"Fuck, I need to be inside you," he groaned against my skin. "I just had you, but I fucking crave you. Always. I'll always crave you." His fingers gripped my ass, stilling my movements as his other hand positioned his cock at my opening. "I'm never going to get enough of you, Wren. Never."

Oh, so slowly, I filled myself with him. At this angle he was so big, so thick, I almost couldn't move. That was until he moved me. One hand on my ass and the other threaded through my hair, he controlled every movement, every thrust, every circle of my hips, lighting a fire in me that made me damn near mindless.

"Look at me, Wren. Open your eyes."

That order was threaded through with so much heat, so much fire, so much power, I had no choice but to look at him. His irises were glowing the gold of his wolf, the animal so close to the surface I could almost see it. It was wild and primal, and the growl that came from him when I met his eyes only solidified that fact.

"Missed you, Bird. Missed you so fucking much."

"I'm not going anywhere," I whispered, the reassurance something he needed, even if he wouldn't say it.

His golden gaze bore a hole in me as I cupped his jaw, kissing his lips as if I'd die if I didn't get another taste. His hold tightened. "Say it again."

I swallowed hard. "I'm not going anywhere." Tears threatened to undo me, but I kissed him again before adding what he really needed to hear: "I'm here. I'm alive. I'm real. I made it back to you and I am never leaving. You hear me, Nico? I'm not leaving you. Not ever again."

And then I wasn't on top anymore. No, he turned us, putting my back on the stone bench, and then he was over me, in me, consuming me until there was nothing left but pleasure and his growls and my moans and his delicious weight on me.

"Again. Tell me again."

And I did. I said it over and over as he wrung my

pleasure from me. He fucked me, made love to me, he bit me, and he made me come over and over until he had to hold me up as he helped me wash up and condition my hair.

I was boneless, well-fucked, and sleepy.

And before I ever got a chance to go down to the Acosta dungeon, I was curled against Nico in his bed, taking a well-deserved nap.

Post shower, a nap, and some new clothes, we finally managed to traverse the wide staircase that led to the Acosta dungeon. And by "we," I meant me, Nico, and the giant wolf he called Ghost. The same wolf that had parked his ass in front of our room like a damn guard dog and apparently took a chunk out of Zaid's ass while Nico and I were busy showering.

The white wolf picked down the stairs ahead of us, sniffing the air like he was scenting for danger. But I didn't expect danger here. Truth be told, it was the nicest dungeon I'd ever seen—especially coming from the Dark Court one. Personally, I'd classify it more like an unfinished basement with dark stone walls and minimal windows. The area was wide open with a single cell at the center. The lighting was soft with pretty sconces dotting the walls to warm up the space. A few dehumidifiers had been set up in the corners to pull the ever-present Savannah moisture out of the air, reducing the dank coldness that should fill a room like this.

But no matter the lighting or the dehumidifiers or the throw pillows, the fact remained the same. It *was* a dungeon, and the woman inside the cell knew it.

Fiona sat on a pretty green velvet couch with rolled arms under a cute throw blanket with frogs on it, her gaze trained on a large TV playing *Legally Blonde* while she filed her nails. Sometime in the last three years, she'd dyed her hair a gorgeous shade of fuchsia, the brilliant color mixed with dark purples and a swath of blue. She had an entire manicure set in front of her, complete with every shade of green nail polish ever made. At her feet was a soft-looking shag carpet, and behind a privacy screen was where I hoped a shower and toilet would be. The room smelled of a little bit of ozone, spent magic, coffee, and one of those cute pumpkin spice candles.

The bars of her cell were a special metal, the power radiating from them practically stinging my skin as I got closer. Not that she heard me. Too engrossed in Elle Woods and the costume party debacle, she didn't even look away from the TV. Her prison guard, though, stared at me like I was a fucking ghost.

Theo Acosta sat in a hard metal folding chair, his jaw twitching as he set the old spy novel he'd been unsuccessfully reading on the ground. Considering the last time I'd seen this guy, he'd put a knife to my throat, I couldn't say I was filled with the warm and fuzzies. Then again, the last person to grab me got set on fire and then cut into ribbons, so I figured I was covered.

Plus, Ghost seemed to hate him, letting out a low growl before settling at Nico's side.

"So, you're what all the commotion was about?" Theo rose to his feet, his head bowed slightly. "I'm glad to see you made it home."

But there was resentment there, too. I could smell it. But Theo wasn't who I was here to see.

I tipped my chin up much like Nico had and turned to the bars. "Hey, Troublemaker, I brought you some food."

Fiona's pink braid whipped behind her back as she turned, but when she stood, she immediately plopped back down. I didn't notice at first since she was in a billowing sweater and baggy pants, but Fiona was gaunt. Like if she were anyone else, I'd make sure she was admitted to a hospital, gaunt.

She put a trembling hand to her forehead, even as a

wide smile flitted across her face. "Did I fall off the deep end again, or am I finally dreaming in this gods-forsaken hellhole?"

Theo shot her a worried glance, his entire body tense before he seemed to consciously relax his shoulders and his jaw. "If you're hallucinating, Cupcake, then so am I."

Cupcake?

When had Theo started calling one of my best friends "cupcake"? And Fiona—save for a scalding glance in his general direction—didn't say a word about it.

Interesting.

Nico hadn't had a chance to fill me in on any supposed mental breaks or why exactly Fiona was in this cell under house arrest or why she was so damn skinny—all of which I really wished he would have at least primed me on. Walking in here blind was not a happy feeling at all.

"I leave for three measly years and the world falls apart," I joked, shaking my head, pasting a wide smile on my face. "Now, I know for a fact these mashed potatoes and gravy are the best I've ever tasted, so you really need to get them while they're hot."

Fiona's eyes misted up. "It's really you? You're really here?"

"In the flesh."

She sucked in a huge breath as tears spilled down her cheeks. "I'm not dreaming?"

Drawing nearer to the bars, the null warding grew more and more painful. "If you need me to pinch you, I can do that, but I'd rather you just take my word for it." I didn't like Fi under wards like this. She could barely handle the ABI school's wards—who knew what these were doing to her? "Now let me in there so I can hug the shit out of you."

I moved to open the door when Theo blocked my way. Smartly, he didn't touch me, but that didn't mean he still hadn't pissed me off.

"I can't let you do that."

My eye actually twitched even as Nico's growl erupted through the dungeon. This bastard had the gall to stand in my way? After he refused to see reason about what Diana was doing, after he put a knife to my throat, after he just sat there and watched Nico nearly lose me?

I don't fucking think so.

"How about you don't *let* me do a gods-damned thing, and you get the fuck out of my way, Theo?"

This close to null wards, who knew what my magic would do, but I had enough ill will to do damage regardless. Nico might have forgiven this piece of shit— which was the only way he would still be breathing—

but I hadn't. And until I heard a damn good apology, Theo could tell me what to do around about never.

"Look, I get it," he said on a sigh. "I fucked up."

My eye twitched again. What was that, the Acosta family motto?

"I'm going to need more than an 'I fucked up.' I'm going to need a damn good reason to not put a knife to *your* throat, make *you* bleed, to make *your* family watch as some bitch damn near cuts your head off. I don't know what you said to Nico to make him forgive your sorry ass, but I'm not him. I'm going to need an actual apology, or so help me, I will rip your insides out and wear your hollowed-out carcass as a motherfucking party dress."

Theo's face drained of color before he took a huge step backward. "That was... graphic."

I leveled him with my most scalding glare. "And also, one hundred percent true."

His head bowed, a wolfy show of deference, but it just made me feel icky. "Look, I would love to say I'm sorry and explain and have everything be peaches and fucking cream, all right?" Theo rubbed at the back of his neck, his shoulders bunching up close to his ears. "But the truth is, until you have your will taken away from you, you can never understand. I didn't want to hurt you. I would never hurt someone's mate. I just co—"

"Stop," I ordered, the fight draining out of me. Because I had an inkling of what it was to be out of control of your own life, unable to sway the most basic path of your life. And if Theo was under an Alpha's order... "Your father?"

Theo nodded, bowing his head further, nearly bending in half. "I'm sorry, Wren. I didn't want to hurt you. None of us did. Well, maybe Santi, but he's come around since you saw him last."

Great. Now I had to forgive him, and I didn't even get to punch anyone. *Rude.* "Forgiven. Though, you still need to get out of my way."

Theo winced and remained immovable. "I—"

"I swear to everything holy, if the word 'let' comes out of your mouth, we're going to have a problem."

"Look," he growled as he moved closer, his voice dropping to a whisper, "you can't go in there. It took ages to get this set up going, and you being here will probably disrupt everything we've built. If you go in there, she's going to want to get out. And if Fiona leaves that cell, the ABI will be on her ass in a heartbeat."

Sure, she was on house arrest, but what had she done to warrant this? What could be so big that the ABI would risk their already-precarious situation to come find her?

Confused, I looked between Nico at my back and

Theo practically bent in half at my front. "What? You planning on leaving her in there forever?"

Theo straightened, his jaw solidifying to granite. "No, I don't plan on imprisoning your friend until the end of time. Just until we figure out how to close the gate to Hell she accidentally opened trying to get your ass from the fucking Fae realm."

If Nico hadn't been at my back right then, I would have stumbled back a step. "I'm sorry, *what*? Someone needs to tell me what the fuck is going on, and someone needs to do it right now."

Nico's arm wrapped around my middle. "It's my fault. Fiona was just trying to—"

"Oh, for fuck's sake," Fiona shouted, drawing all our attention. "The only one to blame is me. It was me and my fool hubris and my need to be right. Had I listened to that Fae fucker just once, I wouldn't be in this mess, but here we are."

She approached the bars, her steps shaky and stilted. "But if what I did means that you're really here and I haven't gone off my nut again, well, I'll take it."

Theo snatched the plate out of my hands, fitting it into a little metal slot that I hadn't noticed in the door. "Eat something." At her raised eyebrow, he tacked on a "Please."

She took the foil-wrapped plate and the wrap of

utensils and sat on the cold floor, not bothering to unwrap either. "I was the one who messed up. I thought your blood would make it a snap to open the Fae gates, and boy, did that come to bite me in the ass. Though, thinking it through, the one we should really be blaming is Margot. Had I known your origins, I would have crafted my spell a little better."

None of this made a bit of sense. "You mean my little jaunt to the Fae realm as a child, or the stars I was born under because the Seelie Queen talked about th—"

"Jaunt to the Fae realm?"

Rolling my eyes, I sat on the floor so I could see her better and Ghost parked his big ass right next to my hip, half-laying, half-sitting on me like a real dog. With nothing for it, I scratched him right behind his ears and he practically melted to the ground next to me, his giant head resting on my knee.

"Evidently, this last one was not my first visit. When I was a kid, my parents always talked about 'the incident' that had me transferring to human school. No one said dick about it being me opening a Fae door and just waltzing right through into the Seelie Queen's throne room. By the time I made it back they just assumed I was dead and moved on with their lives."

That bit still hurt—them forgetting about me—but it wasn't at all surprising. And it made sense that her spell went sideways on her. If I indeed was a Fae-realm-walking, door-busting freak, that was information everyone needed to have before a spell was cast to bring me home.

Variables and all that.

But the longer the silence stretched, the more I realized Fiona wasn't talking about that. No, she was talking about something else.

"Why do I get the feeling I'm not going to like what you're about to tell me?"

Fiona winced just like Theo had, fiddling with the napkin around her utensils. "After you were taken, that Fae fucker locked down all the doors to the realm. No one could get in or out, meaning you couldn't get out even if you tried."

This I knew. Tristan had told me before locking me in, leaving me to the whims of his father as a distraction.

"But he disappeared, and we had to find him. The first order of business was finding the illusion mage who made the deal with him to get his daughter back. And after we had his name, we could summon him. Unfortunately, I didn't have enough power to summon him on my own—not for months. We called in favors, made deals, did everything we could just to get him." She shook her head, her shoulder drooping. "But when we got him, he wouldn't talk. Wouldn't do anything but sit there and wait us out. So, I… got creative."

Fiona hugged her legs to her chest as if she were freezing, and I had the strongest urge to rip the door off its hinges and put a blanket around her shoulders.

"If I didn't have the power to open the door myself, and if Nico couldn't break him, and if that pixie dust motherfucker wouldn't do what was right, then I thought I could borrow his power and do it, anyway. And it worked. Sort of. I opened a door all right. I just opened the wrong fucking one."

"Okay, but the door you opened in Chatham Square?" I clarified to her reluctant nod. "Is the one I came through, so you didn't open the wrong one. You made it so I could come home. But I'm fuzzy on why my origins make a difference or why the city is on literal fire."

Granted, the Fae realm had damn near been breaking apart by the time I'd left, but still. And getting out meant I'd left everyone behind. The number still rang in my head. Forty-four. Well, forty-three now with Lewis free.

"Because she didn't open a door to the Fae realm," Nico answered, kneeling at my side. "She opened a door to Hell. That's why there are demons all over Savannah. It's why the ABI is trying their best to contain the city.

Why if they ever figure out Fiona is the source of the power that opened it, she isn't just going to be on house arrest. She'll be dead."

Theo plopped back onto his folding chair. "You skipped the part about Zephyr. I really want to see her face when you tell her she's kin to a Prince of Hell."

I was glad I was sitting down because the world spun a little and I held onto Ghosts fur like I'd spin off the planet at any second. "Excuse me?"

"Way to go, dipshit," Fiona grumbled, watching my face like a hawk.

Nico stood, smacked his brother upside the head and then continued his crouch by my side. "When Fiona opened the gate, a demon walked out of it. A Prince of Hell. He claims he is your kin, but in demon-speak that could mean anything. He's been reluctant to spill the details, only that when you came home, he would like to meet you."

There had been many a time in my life where I had avoided the truth to save my sanity. Where I would bury a problem so far down deep that it just didn't exist anymore. Unfortunately, this was one of the times that I had to face a problem head-on.

Because one moment, there were just the five of us in this dungeon, and the next, there was a giant, redheaded demon sitting on a leather wingback like he'd been there the whole time, his curled black horns reaching for the ceiling.

Aww, come on. I haven't even been back a full damn day.

"Hello, my kin," the demon said, his smile wide and his gaze calculating.

Nope. There was no getting out of this one.

CHAPTER 10

NICO

The last time Zephyr arrived unexpectedly, the majority of Savannah's historic district burned. If it weren't for a boatload of spells that kept the fire semi-contained to Chatham Square, there would be nothing left of my home or any other building in Savannah. A part of me felt responsible for the mess—especially considering I supplied the blood and the Fae asshole required for said spell—but the other part laid the blame at the feet of Desmond's fuckhead of a son.

The Prince of Hell seemed nice enough, but I knew better than to ever trust a demon. I had met many incorporeal demons in my days in the ABI and dealing with them had never been my favorite. Demon deals were more than frowned upon by not just the ABI, but all councils save the one in Flagstaff for some reason.

For one, demons were wildly mercurial, and twisting a contract was their favorite pastime. Two, possessions were sticky business—exorcisms even more so. I'd only heard of one person surviving without serious mental damage, and word on the street was that she wasn't even wholly arcane but a demigod just walking amongst us.

I didn't know how Savannah was going to survive with the multitude of demons just walking around like it was an amusement park or how we could possibly exorcise that many people without killing them all.

But that was a problem for another day.

Finding my feet, I scooted Wren behind me—not that it would help. If Zephyr wanted to be somewhere, all he had to do was snap his fingers and he was there. There was no ward and no spell that could keep him out. At least none that could be created by anyone on this planet.

That didn't stop Ghost from growling at him or putting his enormous body in between us and the prince.

Shall I bite him, Alpha?

Rolling my eyes, I shook my head. *No, Ghost. He is not a threat.*

Lies. He is made of dark things. He is all threat.

"Hello, Zephyr. How can I help you?"

The giant demon tilted his head to the side, ignoring my pleasantries. His gaze was locked on Wren—the whole reason he had stayed in Savannah in the first place.

"You can stop hiding my kin, Alpha. She is in no danger from me. In fact, I aim to save her from those who would do her harm."

"Sweet Mary, please tell me this dude is not my dad," Wren griped, getting to her feet. She skirted around me and Ghost, closer to danger instead of running from it. "No offense to you, but my mother is already Satan's mistress. I do not need an actual demon as my sperm donor. And if you are actually my dad, I'm going to need you to lie to me on this one."

Zephyr's face split into a wide grin, his gaze soft as he stared at my wife. "I do not need to lie. I would never lay with a woman like Margot Bannister. No offense to you, but I have met Eldritch demons with more soul than that woman."

Wren tried to cover her mouth, but the laugh still echoed through the dungeon like the half-crazed witch cackle it was.

"So, you're acquainted." She schooled her features, refusing to back down an inch. I found it sexy as fuck and equally batshit crazy at the same time. She didn't know Zephyr from Adam, and still, she stood tall like an Alpha.

"Quite. And I will say the entire Bannister line is something of a case study in Hell. They use them to teach the young demons how to be petty."

I just fucking bet they do.

If there were ever a family with too much mean in them, it was the Bannisters.

"But the real question is why you have caged the witch? Did she do something she shouldn't?" He tilted his head to the side before snapping his fingers, the bars to Fiona's cell disappearing into thin air. "That's better."

"What the fuck do you think you're doing?" Theo growled, putting himself between Zephyr and Fiona. Hell, he did one better and picked her right up off the floor like she weighed nothing and herded her behind him like he was protecting something precious. "She needs that cage so the ABI doesn't cut her fucking head off, you asshole. Put it back."

Zephyr's form shimmered a little, the scales on his neck rippling as his jaw solidified. "You're the one who stuck her in a cage. Did you not realize you were killing her. Little by little every day, she was dying. And now she is not. Maybe now she can eat without vomiting it all back up five minutes later."

He directed his gaze back to Wren. "You were right to want her out from behind those bars. Your instincts will hone with time, but you need to listen to your gut more. Don't let that dreadful woman's voice ring in your head. Yes?"

Wren's lips pursed like she was trying not to cry. "Why don't *you* get out of my head?"

The big man shrugged, tapping at his temple. "Can't. I am aware of my kin at all times. Your voice is loud."

"It's still rude. If you can't shut it out at least don't comment on it."

She wasn't wrong.

"No, rude would have been to show up when you were indisposed. Rude would have been interrupting your *reunion*. You ate, you showered, you enjoyed your partner. I've waited long enough, and I will have your attention."

"Whoa," I growled, looping my finger into her belt loop and tugging her behind me. "Number one, it is creepy as fuck that you know that shit. And two, some things are inside thoughts."

Wren shuddered. "And here I thought my mother was intrusive."

"Speaking of your mother," Zephyr began before snapping his fingers once more.

A moment later it felt as if someone had taken a hook to my middle, yanking me through space and time and dumping us all in the parlor of a stuffy house that had seen better days. Wren scrambled back, bumping into me, her breaths sawing in and out of her lungs in a panic.

"Why would you bring me here?" she hissed, her gaze darting to every corner of the room like she'd get attacked at any minute.

And that said nothing to the panic flooding our connection. On instinct, I stepped in front of her, pulling her behind me just like Theo had with Fiona. We needed to get them both out of here.

Because there was only one place on this earth that Wren would fear, and unfortunately, it was where she had spent the most time.

"Don't worry, youngling. There is nothing to fear from this place anymore," Zephyr practically cooed, standing from his makeshift throne like he was going to fix years' worth of psychological trauma with a single bullshit platitude.

Ghost didn't like it at all. He braced himself between our little huddle and the demon like he was seriously considering taking a chunk out of him.

"Yeah, right," she scoffed, her anger getting the better of her as she ignored the wolf and me and everything else. "You know nothing of what these people put me through."

His scales rippled again, a sign that the demon was not happy with the way this conversation was going. "I have an idea. And since it is my fault, I am here to make it right."

"Your fault?"

Zephyr sighed before turning, his giant hand gesturing to us to follow. "If you want the story, you're going to have to trust me just a little. Follow me."

I met Wren's eyes, uncertainty filling her more and more by the second. Then all at once, her face blanked, she firmed her jaw, and she gave me a jerky nod. Only then did I take a single step forward.

Fiona made to follow us, but Theo pulled her back. "I don't think so, Cupcake. The ABI will be here any second. I—"

Another cracking snap, and Theo was following Zephyr like a mindless automaton. As funny as it was, I did not like one of my pack getting forced to do anything, and Prince of Hell or not, he wasn't going to hurt my brother.

My growl was long and low, making Wren, Fiona, and Zephyr freeze. "Let him go. No one takes his will away. Not *ever* on my watch."

Zephyr sighed. "This is not going how I planned at

all." He snapped his fingers once more, giving Theo control of his body again. "The ABI isn't looking for you, Fiona. They believe the Bannister family were the ones to open the portal. There is no need to hide. You're *welcome*. Now"—He paused, eyeing Theo like he'd really enjoy squishing him underneath his big leather boot—"do you want answers, or do you want to stay in the dark?"

Fiona steeled her back, her gaunt frame hurting my very soul. "Oh, you bet your ass, I'm coming."

Wren held out her hand and Fiona took it, my wife funneling power into her friend so fast it was like watching a balloon inflate. Her cheeks filled out as her spine straightened. Fiona's color returned, and she took her first easy breath in years. I might have been able to heal someone, but Wren could restore power like I never could.

But I felt Wren's nose bleeding before she did. The scent of her blood filled my nostrils, and it took everything I had in me not to shift. My wolf was so close to the surface, it was physically painful to keep him locked down. Wren let Fi's hand go to wipe the red away and I felt myself lose it a little.

"You planning on teaching her how to combat that little hurdle?"

You asshole, I tacked on inside my head because it

needed to be addressed. All this drama, and he was walking around like he was the king of the fucking universe.

Zephyr studied Wren for a moment. "You aren't drawing on the earth like you should, or the ether. You are breaking your own body down to give it away, and while I appreciate the sentiment, you need to stop."

Wren gnashed her teeth. "You and that damn Seelie Queen keep saying the same thing, but you don't explain it, you don't tell me what that means. Draw from nothing, from liminal spaces, draw from fucking what? It makes no sense."

The prince studied her a bit. "Did they teach you nothing?"

Wren's eyes started glowing. "Why would they teach me anything? I was their battery, not their equal. I was the fuel for their spells, not their family, not their blood. You call me your kin, but what exactly am I to you? I'm not your daughter, not your cousin, not your anything. I didn't see you waltzing in here when my mother locked me in a fucking closet for spilling a glass of chocolate milk. I was five. You know how long I was in that closet? Two days. Covered in vomit and piss and shit because I was so scared."

Her palm lit, that same fire she'd used on the Fae who wanted to kidnap her. She pointed to the closet in question, and I wanted to rip it apart plank by plank.

"Where the fuck were you when she didn't speak to me for a month after I accidentally set the lawn on fire because she did a spell too close to me? Do you know what that does to a child? No one would speak to me— not my parents, not my aunts or cousins, not my grandmother. I was seven. No 'I love you,' no 'good night,' not one word. Eventually I stopped talking, too. I brought home straight A's, and it didn't matter. I broke things. I begged. Nothing mattered. She didn't talk until I was good enough for long enough. If it weren't for Ellie and Alice, I would have gone insane. If I'm your kin, where the fuck were you?"

I knew the day would come when I would rip every single member of Wren's family apart. It looked like today was the day. Without much thought to the flames building in my wife's palm, I wrapped an arm around her middle, and dropped a kiss to her shoulder.

"I'll be your family, Bird. I'll make sure you're safe and loved. That nothing like that ever touches you again."

But that was the thing about pain like that. It was always there, hiding, waiting. Ready and willing to lash out at any moment. I'd never be able to erase what her parents had done. It didn't matter if they were cold in the ground or alive and well. The scars on Wren's heart were here to stay. The only thing I could promise was that if we ever decided to have kids, nothing of the sort would ever touch them, either.

The pain and rage and hurt filled her heart as she swallowed hard. A moment later the flame in her palm went out.

Zephyr's face split into a smile. "Control. You've learned it so quickly. I'm impressed."

"I don't give a shit if you're impressed. I care about knowing who and what I am and learning to master whatever power I've got. Can you do that or are you going to leave me to the wolves?"

He considered her, his black eyes calculating as they looked her over. "Fair enough. Follow me."

Zephyr led us through Wren's childhood home. At one time it must have been beautiful. The dark mahogany floors and expensive sconces and plush carpets had all seen better days. Dust coated everything along with a heavy layer of debris. Broken bottles and food wrappers and pages from grimoires littered the ground.

Someone was living here—had to be.

"They thought their wards were good enough, but hubris will get people like that every time." He snapped his fingers, revealing a hidden door in one of the beaten-up wooden panels. It exposed a staircase that led to a darkness that had the hair on the back of my neck standing up.

Something had died down there. Something or someone.

"Please tell me there is a point to this," I growled, clutching Wren to my back as I moved away from the door.

There were dungeons and then there were *dungeons*. No way was I subjecting Wren to whatever it was down there without a damn good reason.

"It is her revenge. Would you deny her that?"

Wren finally getting revenge? No, I wouldn't deny her.

I'd help her dig their fucking graves.

There were plenty of things I wanted. A stable home life. A good place to live. Food on my plate and clothes on my back. Friends. People I could call family and mean it.

But revenge had never been on that list.

Of course, I loathed my family. I hated what they'd done to me—the way they'd made me feel. I hated their power and their complete disregard for people around them disguised as "just the way we do things." I hated the way they would step on anyone—even their own blood—to get what they wanted.

But all I'd ever wanted was to be free.

"I don't need revenge," I whispered, the truth of that statement questionable at best. It was the right answer, though—even if it wasn't honest. But making my family pay for their crimes was laughable. I'd already taken all my power back. I'd ripped their power source away from them, and by the looks of this place, I powered the whole fucking house.

What more could I do to them than that?

"The fuck you don't," Fiona hissed. "I showed you basic kindness and you acted like I was giving you the most precious gift. I treated you like a person, and it was as if you'd only gotten that round about never in your life. Day in and day out for how many years have you been alive now?"

I waggled my hand. "Twenty-four-ish years, but I don't know the date anymore. I could be twenty-eight by now."

Fiona planted her fists on her hips, giving me the full hip-jut and stomping foot. "Not the fucking point and you know it. Stop changing the subject. And if you won't do it for revenge, do it for me. Those bitches need to take the fall for the Hell gate fiasco, and dead bitches are much easier to pin shit on than live ones."

That was... fair. Not that I thought I could kill anyone. Plus, I still didn't want to go down to that rancid dungeon. Nico's little power boost made my sense of smell bulletproof, and I was paying for it now.

"There better be nose bleach after this," I grumbled, tipping my chin at Zephyr to lead the way.

Of all the places he could have brought me, here was the absolute dead last one I wanted to ever visit. In fact, I'd sort of made a promise to myself after they'd unceremoniously thrown me to the mercy of the council that I would never darken their door again in my life. Mentally, I'd cut them off, and after Eloise's tantrum up in Blue Ridge, I was more than done with my family. Had I known it was like cutting off a limb, I would have used a sharper knife.

Zephyr ducked, his horns nearly scraping the stone ceiling as he moved down the stairs. Reluctantly, Nico followed, his hand securely wrapped around mine as his thumb made a circuit over the inside of my wrist. If I didn't know better, I would believe he was trying to assess my pulse, but I did.

The beat of his heart thrummed in my chest just as much as mine did in his.

The stone steps were slick with condensation, proof no one had thought of a dehumidifier or even so much as a can of air freshener. And despite our less-than-stealth descent into this pit of darkness, no one attacked, spelled, or maimed us, but I had a feeling that was too good to be true.

There was no way this place shouldn't be warded out the ass. There should be sigils on every exposed surface of the stone—both hidden and exposed—but all

I saw was a blank wall. This had a wonky feeling to it, the same as the circumstances that got me spirited away to the fucking Fae realm.

"I don't like this. This isn't right," I hissed at Nico's back. "No wards, no protection. This is fucked, man."

Illusion magic, my brain supplied, and that had my feet freezing to the spot. I'd already gotten fucked by illusion magic once and not in the good way. Fiona squeezed my hand, probably to agree, but I couldn't look at her. I was too busy keeping my head on a swivel, waiting for shit to go pear-shaped.

At the base of the stairs were three curved paths cut from a rough rock wall, the cave of a dungeon branching out into what seemed like nothingness. Now, I had lived in this house my whole life. Not once did I ever expect that we had a damn labyrinth underneath the floorboards. Again, not good. Three directions meant three chances to die.

I really didn't want to die right now. I had a hot husband, no one in the pack wanted to kill me at the moment, and I'd had roughly a zillion orgasms today, which was a solid improvement from Fae imprisonment from yesterday. Life was on an upswing.

It just figured shit would go straight to Hell in a hand basket.

But it wasn't until we reached the antechamber

right before the paths, did shit really go sideways. Fiona —being the only one of us who couldn't see in the dark —snapped her fingers. And just as that pretty pink flame bloomed in her hand like a rose, spells came at us from all sides.

Theo grabbed Fiona, ducking back into the stairwell while Ghost and Nico stood in front of me like they could block every spell with their bodies alone, the pair of them growling like the sound would do something. And Zephyr practically giggled as he flicked orbs of electricity and fire away from him, batting them like a cat would a particularly interesting toy.

An orb of electricity hit Nico, knocking him sideways and slamming him into the stone wall, and I realized I was just about done with this shit.

Áine and Zephyr had both said that I could take energy into myself, that I could pull it from space and time and use it to fuel my magic. I'd been scolded twice in twenty-four hours about the same damn thing.

No time like the present to see if they were pulling my leg.

The magic called to me, damn near begging me to take it. Just like in the Fae dungeon, I used that sound to my advantage. Focusing on the ringing of the power itself, I pulled it to me, damn near plucking the magic out of thin air and consuming it.

An orb I missed hit Ghost, another hit Nico, burning them both. Nico let out a pained grunt and Ghost whined, and my rage got the better of me.

Roughly, I yanked at the power in the room, consuming it, eating it, sucking it dry until I reached the tipping point. Then a scream ripped from my lips as I gave it all back. Rivers of fire flew from my fingertips, snaking down the three paths like a damn tsunami, coating everything. No one—no spell, no witch was surviving that unless they were gods-damned fireproof.

By the time the flames petered out, I was a shaky mess on my knees, but no more spells materialized from the depths of those fucking paths, and that was a win in my book.

Zephyr's paw of a hand hauled me to my feet, but I didn't have the energy to deal with him.

Nico. I need Nico.

Bleary and unsteady on my feet, I ignored everything and stumbled to my husband.

"Jesus, fuck, Bird," he rumbled, his arms closing around me like I was something precious.

"Are you hurt? Is Ghost okay?" The room was getting darker, and I didn't know why. "I need a nap, I think. I'm tired."

Nico lifted me off my feet—probably before I fell—snarling at Zephyr when he tried to touch me. "This is your fucking fault. Bringing her here—letting them hurt her again—this is your doing and I swear if she—"

"I'm fine," I mumbled, patting his chest. Or at least I thought it was his chest. Shit was a little fuzzy right then.

"Sweet Pea, your ears are bleeding," Fiona sassed. "If you'd admit you're a little more than not fine that would be awesome. No offense, but this stoic, Alpha's wife bullshit is already getting old."

Tell me about it.

"I just need a nap."

"You need a fucking keeper," Theo grumbled. "You two never heard of ducking and letting the giant demon prince handle shit? I thought you were supposed to be her mate not her charge, little brother."

Nico hugged me to his chest. "Fuck you, Theo."

"Yeah, yeah. Fuck me and you're the one who let her stand there and—"

I peeled open an eyelid, not sure when I closed it. "Fuck you, Theo."

A cold nose poked my cheek at the same time a very sharp claw tapped my forehead. Somehow, I peeled both lids open to spot a very put-out Zephyr eyeing me like I was a test to his sanity.

"I stand corrected. You do not have even the smallest inkling of control. You do, however, have an anger problem and the power to strip an entire compound of magic, so, well done there. Here," he said on a sigh, pressing the pad of his finger against my forehead. "This should fix it."

And then a power unlike I'd ever felt filled me, fixing things I had no idea were even broken. Like with Nico, I actually felt wounds closing and blood drying. I felt organs repair themselves and blood replenish. It was fucking wild.

But then an awareness hit me, making me scramble to my feet and a wash of fire hit my palm.

Whatever I had done, it hadn't killed everyone down here. Hell, it likely hadn't killed anyone at all.

"Someone is down here. Two... no, three."

What I didn't say was how many dead bodies lined those three paths. People long since dead, and not by my hand, which wasn't quite the relief it should have been.

"Yes, well," Zephyr murmured, snapping his fingers.

As if pulled by a string, three women flew from their paths, colliding in a heap at Zephyr's feet. Another snap later, and a black ring encircled them before glowing red with an unspent fire.

"That's enough spells from you three. Wren, my dear, say hello to the last three Bannister witches on the planet."

I opened my mouth to correct him, but he held up a finger.

"You are not a Bannister witch. As someone who has never been inducted into their coven, any claim you have to that name ended when you married into the Acosta pack. Therefore, any curses, spells, or debts— soul or otherwise—of the Bannister name do not affect you."

Respecting this line of thinking, I snapped my fucking mouth closed and paid attention. My grandmother, Eloise, my aunt Judith, and my mother were sprawled in a tangle of limbs. It sort of made sense that they would be the last ones standing—or at least living, as it were.

Eloise shoved away from her daughters, climbing to her feet as if all three hundred years had finally caught up with her. The last time I'd seen her, she had looked no older than forty at a push. Now, she could pass for a grandmother to one of the *Golden Girls*. Hell, the only reason I even knew it was her was the stuffy, bitchy, insult that fell out of her mouth as soon as she saw me.

"Well, if it isn't the screw-up and her mongrel. What? You come to finish us off, you ungrateful little bitch?"

I should have expected something like that, but the insult still hurt. I wasn't the one who'd stolen power not meant for her. I wasn't the one who'd done everything to make me feel unwelcome. I wasn't the one who'd broken her family.

No, that was on them.

Nico's growl shivered down my spine as he yanked me behind him. "You'd better think up a spell to shut them up, demon, or else they won't live long enough to play out whatever bullshit scenario you brought us here for. They insult my wife again and I'm ripping their tongues from their heads. You understand me?"

Zephyr's smile was practically beatific. "I like you. You're a good husband and protector. I approve." His attention shifted to Eloise. "Your input is no longer needed. You may stay silent now."

Ghost circled the spelled ring, his growl growing louder by the second while the three women remained silent.

"Now, I brought you here so you could have your mother tell you how you came to be, but seeing how they treat you, I'm not sure this was a good idea," Zephyr mused, tapping his chin.

Theo threw up his hands. "Ya *think*? Perhaps you should ask people before you transport them places and make them relive childhood trauma, maybe?" Nico's brother was telling the complete truth. "Fuck, man, are you new or something?"

I couldn't help it: I snorted a laugh that was one-part hysterical and one-part pure joy. Because Nico's brother was indeed scolding a likely ancient, most definitely god-level-powered Prince of Hell like he was a naughty puppy. I'd never met someone with a bigger death wish.

"I should have kept you mindless, wolf. Your mouth is going to get you into trouble one day."

"That's what they tell me." Theo's smile was as wide as it was patronizing. "And yet, I'm still here."

As funny as it was, this wouldn't get me the fuck out of this dungeon anytime soon. "Can we get back on task, please? How I came to be? The whole sordid tale—can we get back to that before I get the black plague from this dank-ass dungeon?"

Zephyr sniffed, his eyebrow raising in indignation before he snapped his fingers. "Margot, why don't you tell us all about the deal you made?"

He said it like a request, but I knew my mother had no choice in the matter.

Margot's eyes narrowed to slits as she stood like she was gearing up to spew enough emotional trauma to power the bank accounts of every therapist in Savannah—maybe even the great state of Georgia as a whole.

"Why else would I summon a demon? Power. Had I

known what I do now, I would have never done it. You failed to hold up your end of the bargain."

If Theo had a death wish, Margot was actively courting Death herself to come rip her soul right out of her body—that was if she even had one.

Zephyr stood to his full height. "I fulfilled every aspect of our deal. It was you who failed to be clear. You asked for power, and I gave it to you. It's not my fault you lost it. You asked for wealth and influence, and had you actually fostered any kind of goodwill, you would have had it for the rest of your days. Instead, you ostracized the one person who could have given you everything you asked for and more."

But I had no idea what that meant.

But Margot was used to my confusion. I didn't have to say a word before she decided to drop a verbal bomb on my life.

"You, my *darling* daughter, are what happens when a demon deal goes south while pregnant."

argot Bannister was the worst mother on the planet.

"Who the fuck makes a demon deal while pregnant?" Fiona asked.

I had to give it to her, that question also blazed across my brain about fourteen times while I stood there gaping at my bitch of a mother.

No. "Bitch" was too nice for Margot. There had to be something worse than that.

I didn't even know what to say to her. Like how could she be so fucking stupid? How could she care about no one but herself?

Margot's gaze sliced to Fiona. "It wasn't like I knew, okay? I was only six weeks along. How was I supposed to know that her father's sperm were impervious to every birth control spell in the book?"

First, gross, and second, there are birth control spells?

Probably not a good idea for me.

I'd probably torch my whole uterus.

"That... actually makes me hate you a little less, and I didn't think that was possible. But a demon deal for power? Even I'm not that stupid and I've done some questionable shit in my day."

Judith stood, her calculating expression the one I needed to watch out for. Out of the three, Judith would kill without a second thought. "Yes, we all know about your penchant for missteps."

The disdain just dripped from her words, but I was on this side of a demon's circle and she wasn't, so...

Margot flipped her matted red curls from her shoulder. In the last three years she had gone from a twinset-wearing, pearl-clutching, Southern Belle to little better than a street urchin. Hell, street urchins were probably cleaner.

"There was no way around it. The Acosta pack was expanding, the Fae wanted payment, and there were some upstart covens trying to take what our family fought and died for. Power was the only way."

Judith snorted. "It should have been me. If we had

gone with the plan as I laid it out, none of this would be happening and yo—"

Eloise's hand cracked against her youngest daughter's face. "It was your thirst for blood that got us in this situation in the first place. You killed that Fae child for spell ingredients. What did you think would happen?"

"Does anyone else have a hankering for popcorn?" Theo mused, his fingers massaging his temples. "Because I know telenovelas with less drama. *Shit.*"

The man was not wrong.

"Does any of this have a point?" I asked Zephyr, trying not to run screaming from the dungeon. I thought my family was bad, but killing kids? Demon deals? Mysterious cave structures and dungeons? *The fuck?*

"It does. You see, Margot made a deal for power, but since her soul is just as black as her sister's, I couldn't in good conscience give it to her directly. Tell me—have you ever played Corrupt a Wish?"

I could honestly say I had not. Loopholes weren't exactly my cup of tea.

"Well, I gave her exactly what she asked for. I gave her power, and when she grew you in her womb, her power grew. But when you were born, she thought she lost it. It wasn't until you fell into the Fae realm, did they even consider that you were amplifying their magic. And when the Seelie Queen brought you back? And the blessings she gave you? Well, it was too late to stop them."

I would have gone my whole life without magic, put down, and cowering if it weren't for Nico's family breaking the curse. I didn't appreciate what they had done to break it or the steps they had taken in deceiving us, but...

"Stop them from what? Cursing me to drain the power you gave me? The power she was promised? Not for nothing, but do you happen to think about the consequences to your actions, or are you a 'fly by the seat of your pants' kind of demon?"

But that didn't mean my family was off the hook, either.

"And you three. All your scheming, all your talk of power, and what do you have? Dirty clothes and janky hair and a gods-damned dungeon in the middle of an apocalypse you probably had a hand in creating. I swear, for all the times you called me a fuck-up, I would like you to look around at your current circumstances and eat your fucking words."

Plus, the only reason I was considered a "fuck-up" at all was due to their bullshit curse.

"That's rich," Judith hissed. "You couldn't even

break my wards with all your *power*, but sure, you're not a fuck-up. A waste is more like it."

Zephyr stepped in between us, staring down at Judith like he would really enjoy burning the flesh from her bones. "And how many sacrifices did you make to strengthen that ward, witch?"

One thing about Judith, she had a spine made of steel. "Evidently not enough since she's still alive, but don't you worry. I'll be sure to do better next time."

Next time? Did she really think that she was getting out of here?

"I thought we discussed this," Nico growled, pulling me away from the circle. "Either end them or I will."

But ending them wouldn't do a damn thing. All they wanted was power, and they didn't have it. What more punishment did they need?

Sighing, I squeezed Nico's hand, tugging it as I tried to head back for the stairs. "I'd like to leave. If you're done with this walk down memory lane, I have about a million places I would rather be."

"I am not done with you, child," Zephyr growled, snapping his fingers. "It is time for your revenge."

I would have screamed that I didn't need it, but that snapping sound was compounded by the ward surrounding the remains of my family breaking.

Oh, fuck.

Margot shot a spell across the now-open space, aiming right for me faster than a lightning strike. Smartly, both Nico and I ducked, but she wasn't alone. I supposed gunning for me was on brand and everything, but I was just so fucking tired of it all.

Tired of them using their limited power to get whatever they wanted. They didn't deserve what they had. They had *never* deserved what they had. They shouldn't have any of it.

Just like their spell from before, I drew from the magic on the air. Only this time? I took it directly from the source. Rage filled me once again as I yanked on their bullshit power—the same power they used to siphon mine from me. The same power that had stolen my happiness, my childhood, my self-worth. The same one that made me feel like a burden, like an idiot, like a touch-starved drain on the Bannister name.

Another scream ripped up my throat once again, only this time it came directly from my soul, unleashing years of pain, of tears, of fear.

And all at once, I drew from them everything that made them witches. Their magic, their knowledge, their potions, their books. I took away their years, their lifespan, their connection to the earth.

I took everything. But I didn't let it fill me. No, I sent it out, away, out of their reach.

"This is what you deserve," I snarled, drawing every single thing away. "To have human years and human lives and human protection—which is none in case you were wondering. You get human health and human fragility. And when you are old and decrepit and begging for death, I want you to remember me. You don't get to just shuffle off this mortal coil. No, death is too good for you. You get to *live*."

Granted, in the middle of the mess of Savannah, their lives might be short, but I wouldn't be the one to kill them. No, I wanted them to live nice long lives with nothing. *That* would be my revenge.

I watched as they remained crumpled at my feet, but the feeling was bittersweet. Even this was unsatisfying, just as all revenge always was. I just wanted to move on with my life.

"Are you sure, child?" Zephyr asked, assessing me with an inscrutable expression. Who knew how old he was or how many times he'd witnessed just the same thing? Who knew what he saw at all when he looked at me? He called me "child" and "kin" but that was only because he made the mistake of ever dealing with Margot at all. "Are you positive you want them to live?"

Rolling my eyes, I crossed my arms over my chest.

"Are you asking me if I want their blood on my hands? Because if so, the answer is no. They cursed me so magic was lost to me. They took more than their fair share. What do you do to a bully who takes and takes and takes? You cut them off so they can't take more. This is enough."

It wasn't enough—it would probably never be enough—but it was all I was willing to do.

"And what if I told you that the reason they are the last Bannisters is not because of outside power grabs and violence, but something else? What if I told you that they killed everyone else and took their power to fuel their spells —even your father, if you can call that man a father at all."

Swallowing, my gut roiled with that new knowledge. Eloise, Margot, and Judith probably all deserved to die. They likely deserved an eternity roasting over a spit. But I wasn't going to be the one to do it.

"Then, I'd say they have plenty of time to think about what they've done while they wait for their turn in Hell."

"Are you fucking kidding me?" Nico rumbled, his eyes glowing with the gold of his wolf. "No. You don't leave a threat free to come back and kill you. They need to die, Wren. Now."

"I took their knowledge, their spells, their books.

They know magic exists but can't reach it. That is enough." I swallowed down a pit of dread that maybe I failed to do this right, too. "They don't get to take my soul away from me. They don't get to kill the last part of me that's good. They have taken *enough*."

My gaze cut to Zephyr. "You can't use me as your weapon, and you can't manipulate me into meting out your revenge. I wasn't the one who made the deal. If you want to punish someone, punish them."

Zephyr's smile was once again equally beautiful and the thing of nightmares. "You surprise me, child. I worried with Margot as your mother, you would be just as debased as she is. Then again, Áine did put an angel in your path, didn't she?" That made not one bit of sense, but Zephyr didn't deign to elaborate. "You, my dear, have passed the test."

With that, he pressed the pad of his index finger against my forehead, sending a searing rip of agony through me. My scream was silent, but I still fell to my knees all the same. If I thought his boost from earlier was good, this was that times a million.

Because everything I tore from my family, every bit of power that I refused to take into myself—the knowledge, the magic, everything—flooded my veins. That, and Zephyr gave me more.

So much more.

I couldn't see anything, but I felt every molecule of the world as it moved around me. Nico held me to his chest as he yanked me from the demon prince, his heartbeat erratic, the breaths in his lungs stilted and full of fear. I felt Theo change into his wolf as Ghost launched himself at the source of my agony.

"Stop it," Fiona screamed, a spell I couldn't see forming in her palm. "You're killing her."

A snap of his fingers later and the room was eerily silent, all except for the demon's voice in my head, soft as a baby's breath.

Soon, you will not feel this pain, and you will understand why I had to test you. I had to know if you deserved the full extent of your power. You may not be my child by blood, but I had a hand in creating you, and you have earned everything I am giving you.

This is protection, my child.

Protection and insurance.

And when you find yourself in need—and you will—please do not hesitate to call on me.

Then all at once, the bright, white-hot agony and Zephyr's voice was gone.

"Bird?" Nico called, gently shaking me. "Baby? Jesus Christ, Wren, are you okay?"

With a sheer force of will, I peeled one eyelid open and then the other to stare into Nico's eyes. The gold irises were filled with so much worry, so much pain, it was as if it touched my very soul. I put a hand to his cheek, the soft hairs of his beard tickling my palm.

With that one touch, it was as if I took years off of him. His brow relaxed as relief hit him, filtering through our bond in a shimmering wave.

"I'm okay. Let's get out of here, yeah?"

I didn't want to see my family ever again, and with the knowledge I'd just absorbed, I would never have to. Hell, if I wanted, I could make it so they couldn't find me even if they were looking right at me. And as pissed as I was at Zephyr for leading us here and then just ditching us, his gift and promise was a decent consolation prize.

Nico pulled me to my feet and pressed a kiss to my temple. "There are some things to button up here first. Go upstairs with Fiona. Theo and I will handle this." He shook his head, his jaw clenching as he surveyed what remained of my family. Eloise was on her knees, clutching her head while Judith was in a ball on the ground, sobbing. Margot kept snapping her fingers, trying to get her magic as silent tears poured down her face.

"What did you do to me? Why is nothing working?"

she muttered to herself, shaking her head as she snapped her fingers over and over again.

Frowning, I pulled my hand out of his and backed away. "There is nothing to 'button up' down here. It's done."

Nico's eye twitched as he set his jaw. "Do you think as your husband, I will let a threat to your life live?"

A cold pit of dread filled me. "What threat? Three sobbing witches with no access to power?"

It was as if I pulled the pin on Nico's rage.

"No access?" he whispered. "No access?" This one was a whole hell of a lot louder. My ears rang as his body seemed to double in size. His wolf—which had been so close to the surface—shimmered behind the features of his face. "Do you honestly believe they can't get *access*? That they can't make a deal with one of the zillion demons running around Savannah or trade with a Fae or summon another coven here?"

I opened my mouth to counter, but he wouldn't let me.

"Never again, Bird. I swore to myself when they took you that I wouldn't let another threat to your life live, and those bitches are a fucking threat."

Without warning, he hauled Judith up by the throat, his fingers squeezing the life out of her. Her feet barely scraped the ground as her fingers clawed at his hand, but he didn't even spare her a glance.

"This one has knives filled with poison all over this house. Did you take all the magic out of those? Did you blank every grimoire and burn every bridge she has? Did you wipe her mind of you?"

Again, I opened my mouth, but I couldn't get a word out before Nico snapped her neck right in front of me. The shock that filled me stuttered the breath in my lungs, and I covered my mouth before a scream ripped from my lips.

Margot scrambled away, staring at her sister as she tried to save her own skin. "I'll stay away. As soon as I can I'll leave Savannah. Please don't kill me."

But Nico didn't so much as *seem* to consider her offer. One second, she was breathing, and the next, her heart was on the floor outside of her body, the squelch of it hitting the stone making my stomach turn.

A moment later Eloise stood, not bothering to look at her fallen children or the man who had every intention of taking her life. Instead, she turned her hateful glare onto me.

"Margot should have killed you the moment she lost her power. She should have snuffed you out like I told her to. Maybe then she wouldn't have had such a stupid, ungratef—"

And then Eloise joined her children on the floor of the dungeon, her head rolling to a stop as her body fell.

I met Nico's golden gaze, his expression not the least bit sorry as he wiped the blood from his sword.

Maybe those three years I'd been gone changed him far more than I knew.

The look on Wren's face cut me to the quick. It was as if she had never seen me before in her life. Funny, she hadn't cared at all when it was the Fae nearly killing her and I'd done the same.

"No one is getting to you again, Bird. Not on my watch."

Her hand fell from her mouth, the white imprint of her fingers against her skin blooming red as anger took the place of shock. But she didn't say a word. Instead, she turned her back on me and marched up the slick stone steps to the main level.

Fiona sighed and followed her, shaking her head. She knew. She knew exactly what it had been like and how brutal life had been. It was kill or be killed. In-fighting, grudges, and outright enemies had made mincemeat of the arcane population of this town. And that was before we fucked up and opened a fucking demon portal.

I couldn't have Wren in one more spec of danger.

Theo shot me an understanding expression as he followed Fiona up. Had his mate been in the same position, he would have done exactly as I had. Only this was Theo. He probably would have dismembered them from the toes up so they could watch as he hacked each bit of them away. I wouldn't call my brother sadistic exactly but hurting someone he loved meant he showed no mercy.

Not ever.

Lunch? Ghost's hopeful voice in my head set my teeth on edge. I had a feeling Wren wouldn't take too kindly to the resident untethered wolf just chowing down on what had once been her family—not that they'd ever treated her as such.

"Absolutely fucking not," Wren yelled down the stairs, the simmering rage in her gut getting the better of her. "You let them rot where they sit, Ghost. No lunch for you."

I couldn't see her face, but the disgust in her voice was enough.

Ghost ducked his head, his worried expression something I'd never seen on his wolfy face.

Yeah, buddy. We're both in trouble.

Sighing, I marched up the stairs behind them, just waiting for my wife to finally lose it. But she didn't. No, she stayed silent as she moved through the house, leading us to a room that had seen better days.

Unlike the rest of the house, this room had cheap furniture and sparse decorations. Covered in layers of dust, it was as if it hadn't been touched in some time. The walls were a dingy baby pink, the paint at least twenty years old, maybe older.

Wren moved to the closet, but instead of finding clothes or whatever it was she was looking for, all that remained was a pair of wire hangers and a fair amount of nothing. She moved to her dresser, only to come up empty, too. Same with the nightstands and under the mattress.

Whatever she was looking for was just... gone.

"Bird?"

Wren straightened, narrowing her eyes at me. "Don't you 'Bird' me, Nico Acosta. I don't want to hear a fucking word out of you for the foreseeable future, you understand me?"

Oh, she was *mad*, mad. *Perfect.*

Taking my life in my hands, I just could not shut my mouth. "I'm not sorry."

A spark of fire ignited in her palm, making my whole

gut clench. "Oh, I know you aren't, and that's the fucking problem. I didn't want their deaths on my conscience, dammit. Now all I can do is feel sorry for women that I absolutely should not feel sorry for. Or maybe I *should* feel sorry for them. What if they could have been better? What if they could have changed? What if that punishment meant they... they..."

But she knew better. She knew it but didn't want to accept it. There was no redeeming those women. There were no redeeming people who would sacrifice their own family for power. There was no bringing them back from that. She'd known it three years ago when she kicked Eloise out of our cabin up in Blue Ridge.

Her family had never cared about her unless it was to use her for power.

Wren stamped her foot before sweeping out of the room. Down the hall, up a flight of stairs, and down another corridor, she entered a library. Filled to the brim with grimoires and photo albums and more leather-bound tomes than I could shake a stick at, she searched high and low for whatever it was she was looking for.

"Wren, honey," Fiona cooed, "if you told us what you needed—"

"Proof," Wren barked. "Proof that they gave a shit. Proof that at one time—maybe when I was a baby—

they cared a little." She opened a photo album, slamming through each page before tossing it aside. She moved to the next. "I'm looking for anything. A picture, a memento, a letter, something that says it's not true. That the knowledge that Zephyr gave me is wrong, that..."

I decided right then and there that Wren needed letters. She needed little notes everywhere that told her how much I loved her. She needed a million pictures. She needed movie tickets and concert stubs and every little trinket in the world.

She'd have a library full of them.

I gave Theo a nod, telling him with a single look that he, Fiona, and Ghost should take a hike. Wren didn't need an audience to this anymore than she needed Zephyr to bring her here in the first place. And ignoring her ire, I got closer, wrapping an arm around her waist from behind as she tore through another fruitless book.

She stiffened as I settled around her but then she melted into me, the fight leaving her. "There's no one left and still this building is just another reminder that they never... they never... not once did they ever love me. It's stupid, but... I want to burn it all down."

I couldn't blame her. If I was in her shoes, I would, too. This huge stately mansion filled with no love, no kindness, no hope. If I had to, I'd hand her the fucking matches.

"Then do it, Bird. Is there a single book in this library you want? A single memory you need?"

She looked around, opening a grimoire only to find blank pages. "I took everything. All their knowledge, the magic out of their potions, I rendered every ingredient and every ward inert. I took it all." She swallowed hard. "I still don't quite know *how* I did it, but I know in my soul there was no magic left for them. I wanted them to suffer. I wanted them to know what it was like without magic. But I didn't want their blood on my hands."

"And it's not." It wasn't. The blood was on my hands, and I held zero remorse for it. "They dug their own graves. So burn it all down if you have to, but let that shit go."

Wren sighed before a flame bloomed over her palm once more. I was still getting used to that flame, but in a way, it made sense. If Zephyr had a hand in how Wren came to be, then the fires that seemed to follow her every move meant that her power had been aching to be one with her since the day she was born.

Hesitantly, she pressed her palm to the blank grimoire. The ancient pages caught fire like dried kindling, jumping from book to book as Wren played with the dancing flames. In what seemed like moments, the entire bookcase was engulfed.

"Time to go, Bird," I murmured in her ear, and when she turned, all the pain of her loss was stamped all over her face. Silent tears fell down her cheeks, and it made me want to kill Margot all over again. Her and Eloise. It made me want to watch as their corpses burned to ash.

But Wren didn't need me to do that. She needed someone—anyone—to give a shit about her. And I'd make sure that every single member of our pack adored her almost as much as I did. She would have family—real family—for the rest of her days.

Wren let me lead her out of the Bannister prison, the fresh night air kissing our skin as the flames raged behind us. But she wouldn't let me lead her back to the pack house. She tugged her hand away as she watched the fire engulf her childhood home. And I had to say, I was glad we were doing this alone.

"We have to close the Hell gate," she murmured, her cheeks drying in the heat of the night and the flames.

If I could have figured out how to do that, it would have been done already. Sure, Zephyr wasn't too bad, and the demons had been the least of our problems, but the massive fire burning in the center of the city wasn't exactly good for tourism.

"I'm aware."

"I know how to do it."

I grabbed her shoulders, spinning her to look at me. "That's great. What do you need? How do we do this?"

Wren winced, her gaze landing anywhere but on me.

"Tell me what's going on, Wren."

Yes, I used every ounce of Alpha in that command, and no, it did not work on my wife one bit.

She spun on a heel, briskly heading to the pack house and ignoring me completely. This was not good. If she didn't want to answer, shit was about to take a turn for the worse.

Silence stretched between us until she walked into the pack house, made a beeline for the kitchen, and finally unearthed a bottle of vodka from the freezer. She flicked off the cap and took a swig directly from the bottle.

When the thing was half-drained, I snatched it from her, my patience at its end.

"Talk. Now."

Her gut churned, making my own nearly cough up my dinner.

"I have to open the Fae gate," she mumbled behind her hand.

I didn't understand. "Okay. And why is that a problem? I don't know how you're going to do it, but—"

"It's a problem because I have a shitty-ass Fae King who would really enjoy squeezing the life out of me after he makes me dance for a million years, I only have a vague idea of how to open said gate, and then I have to close the Hell gate. All without dying. Plus..."

Plus? There was a plus in there?

"There are women to save in that fucking Fae prison and I can't go back there without ripping the whole realm apart. And I need Desmond's son to help."

Wren snatched the bottle back from my loose fingers and took it with her as she skirted around me and headed for our bedroom. Did she honestly think I was just going to let that shit go?

"You want me to just sit idly by while you seek out this kind of—"

We were only halfway up the staircase, so when she turned and speared me with a glare that was so incendiary, I was surprised it didn't have actual fire coming out of it.

"I don't want you to sit idly by, Nico. I want you to understand that this isn't the way. Hell gates and Fae gates and demented kings and spoiled princes. Don't you miss the way our home used to be? I've been home for less than a day, and even I know this isn't how it's supposed to work."

She took a swig of vodka.

"But somehow in all this mess, I am somehow the fucking chosen one. I've never been chosen for a damn thing my whole life or managed to not fuck shit up at any point, but sure."

Malia and Hannah peered down at us from the top landing while Fiona and Theo peeked around the corner. I could practically feel the rest of the house listening in while also trying to give us a modicum of privacy.

Wren sensed them, too, and weaved through the growing crowd to our room. On the other side of the door, she set the bottle down. Her back turned, she stared out the window, not even looking at me.

"You can't protect me from everything and everyone, Nico. I'm not a bird you can cage or a princess you can put on a pedestal. I'm just me—a little more than I was before, but I'm just Wren. I'm a clumsy, semi-witch with a job to do. And as much as I don't want to do it, it needs to get done."

I had a feeling I was not going to like this at all.

Sleeping was not in the cards for me.

If it wasn't the totally insurmountable fact of what I was supposed to do, it was Zephyr's bevy of knowledge that he'd just decided to drop on my head. Every moment, more and more of it filtered through my brain. Ancient spells, a library full of grimoires' worth of information—all of it carved out space in my brain.

Before dawn, I finally said, "fuck it" and decided to do something about it. Only, I knew better than to just leave the bed without letting Nico know. Trying and failing to sleep beside him the night before, I got to see his face calm, his brow unfurrowed, and the years I had been gone leave his expression. Tristan's gate idiocy had damn near killed him.

He hadn't known if I was alive, or if I was hurt. He had spent years of waiting, of worrying, or slowly going mad. I saw it every few seconds—the way his gaze darted to me. It was almost as if he was reassuring himself that he hadn't dreamed it.

That I was real.

That I was home and safe—or as safe as he could make me.

But as much as I wanted him to have me safe—as much as I wanted to ease his worry—I had to actually *be* safe. Zephyr's knowledge provided more cautionary tales than I could shake a stick at, but the most important one was how unstable Hell gates were. How easily they can be overrun by souls trying to escape Hell.

How simple it was to tear apart the fabric of our reality.

I had already been doing it in the Fae realm. I wondered how soon it would be before that gate fucked everyone and everything over here.

By the nearly imperceptible tremors I'd been feeling since I set foot back in Savannah, the answer was soon.

I left a note on my pillow after kissing Nico's cheek.

Downstairs. Don't worry. I love you.
—W

And I did love him. I loved him so much, I could forgive a lot of shit. Watching him kill the last members of my family was a big pill to swallow, though. I kept putting myself in his shoes. If his family had done what mine had, would I let them live? Would I not do just as he had?

I probably would. Pretty sure I wouldn't have done it right in front of him, though.

Finding Ghost right outside our bedroom door, I clucked my tongue for him to follow. At the very least, Nico *might* not shit a kitten if I had wolfy backup.

The house was quiet as I padded down the stairs. I needed books—blank ones—and I needed them now.

"Well, look who's back causing trouble," a smooth Southern voice said, stopping me in my tracks.

My gaze darted to the entryway chair at the base of the staircase. Nico's friend Wyatt sat with his hand around a mug of coffee, one ankle resting on his knee. His cowboy boots and western-style shirt seemed at odds with the blond hair obscuring the side of his face and the casual nature he was affecting.

No, this Wyatt was harder than the man I'd met before, his stare less jovial, his jaw tighter.

He tipped his chin at my hand, as he brushed the hair from his face, revealing a gnarled scar spanning the whole of his cheek and down his neck into the collar of his shirt. "That's new."

Looking down, I realized my hand was engulfed in flames. "Oops. It is. It seems to pop up when I'm startled. I'll... get the hang of it."

I hope.

Concentrating, I willed the fire away, and by some miracle, it actually listened to me. "See?"

"Your mate know you're galivanting about? I sorta figured he'd be surgically attached to you for the rest of forever." He sent me a censuring eyebrow raise as he sipped his coffee.

I waggled my now-fire-free hand. "I left him a note. I tried waking him up, but I don't think he's slept right in years. Waking him when he was that peaceful just seemed wrong, you know?"

Plus, I had shit to do before the whole of the world went tits-up. *You know, priorities.*

"If you say so."

I raised my own eyebrow. "How patronizingly noncommittal of you, Wyatt."

At my ire, Ghost showed the big man his teeth. All of them. No growl, but the goal was achieved when Wyatt held his hands up in surrender.

Good puppy, I thought, chuckling to myself.

Ghost straightened and leveled me with a wolfy glare fit for instant death. *I am not a pup. Ghost is ancient.*

"Whoa, now, I didn't mean anyth—"

But I ignored Wyatt to respond to Ghost.

"All dogs are puppies. Old dogs are puppies, puppies are puppies, and even ancient, spirit-ripped wolves who do awesome things are good puppies. Take a compliment, Ghost."

Not a pup.

"*Fine.* I will never call you a puppy again, you temperamental beast."

Ghost's ears perked up. *Beast. I like beast. Call me a good beast.*

I snickered. "Beast it is."

"Ho-ly *shit*," Wyatt said, climbing to his feet. "You can talk to that thing? I thought only Nico could communicate with Ghost."

I shrugged, not understanding it in the least. "Yeah, well, it was a surprise for all of us." But back to the matter at hand. "You got any books around here. Preferably blank ones. Journals? Something?"

I needed to get the information written down before it fell out of my brain, and I lost it all. Okay, that was the lie I was telling myself. Worry churned in my gut—had ever since I got back. At the beginning, it was because I was running through apocalypse world with an open

Hell gate. Though, considering what had come out of it, it wasn't too bad.

Now it was because I knew what *could* come out of it if we left it open too long.

"Maybe in Tomás' old office, but no one has been in there in years. Not since..."

Wyatt hesitated, following us as I pivoted on a heel and headed for the absolute last place I ever thought I'd go. Tomás' office hadn't changed much since the last time I'd been here. Sure, the carpet was stained with my blood and every surface was covered in about three inches of dust, but it was the same.

And here, class, is where Diana tried to cut off my head. And here is where Nico fought his brothers, and here is...

Shuddering, I rubbed my arms. I couldn't believe they hadn't touched it. Not once. It was like the whole house was constantly reliving the same shame I felt right then, and I hated it.

"You might want to stand back," I ordered over my shoulder, using every bit of Nico's Alpha to my advantage. I didn't see so much as sense Wyatt take three healthy steps back, placing himself across the threshold and into the foyer.

Other than the dungeon—a place I did not care about in the slightest—or under duress, I had never done a spell at all. But this room needed me to change it. It needed me to make it right. Concentrating, I saw the room as it should be—expanding it, making it bigger, wider, filling it with tomes and spells and an apothecary's worth of ingredients. When I opened my eyes, I snapped my fingers.

At first, nothing happened. Not a single book moved, or cobweb vanished.

But two seconds later, it was as if the whole place got the *Fantasia* treatment. The chandelier that had sat shattered on the ground for years reassembled itself before reattaching to the ceiling. The desk mended, and the sullied papers arranged themselves in a stack at the corner. The chairs sucked all their fluff back in as the bloodstains disappeared and the fabric stitched back together.

Books flew from one side of the room to the other, stacking neatly on the shelves. The dust and cobwebs melted away as the wall expanded, making the room twice as tall and three times as wide. Tables sprung up out of nowhere with little green library lamps and comfy rolling chairs. Wide plush seats fell from the ether, landing in cute little groups.

And stacks and stacks of books filled the shelves, each one full to bursting with the knowledge I so feared would leave my head for good.

Because closing the Hell gate was going to be risky.

Opening the Fae one even more so, and even as awful and unconscionable as my family was, the knowledge should not be lost. I couldn't be the only one who had it.

"Did I get slipped a roofie when I wasn't looking?" Wyatt muttered, daring to walk into the room now that the conjuring had settled down. "Or did you just *bibbity, bobbity, boo* your ass a whole new library?"

I leaned over and sniffed his coffee. "I'm pretty sure the second one, but I've thought I was dreaming since yesterday, so I wouldn't call myself an expert on reality at the moment."

It was as if I hadn't said a word.

"And where did all these books come from?"

I pulled the first one off the shelf, inspecting it. Indeed, it contained my great-grandmother Gertrude's account of the vampire wars of 1723 and the spells she used to drive the bloodsuckers back.

"My brain," I said on a sigh, the relief hitting me.

I performed a spell.

And it worked.

I didn't know exactly *how* it worked, but it had. And that was one less thing to worry about as we moved forward.

"Quick and dirty version? I stole every ounce of knowledge from the last remaining Bannister witches. Every spell, every memory of magic, every sordid tale. I had to put it somewhere. So..." I held out my hand gameshow-host-style. "Here we are."

But looking at the place now, I wondered if I may have overstepped. There had to be a reason no one touched this space. Sure, Nico's father was dead, but maybe they left it in memory of him.

"Do you think Nico is going to be mad I turned his father's office into my own personal library? Worse, do you think Cat—"

Wyatt shot me a sharp look. "No. Not even a little."

That was emphatic. "Okay. If you're sure. I just didn't want to—"

Wyatt's look only got darker.

"What?"

"Just a question, but have you talked at all about what happened when you left or how Nico became the Alpha?"

I nearly laughed but managed to hold it in at the last second. Between alley sex, dinner, shower sex, a nap, meeting Zephyr, and the Bannister family bonfire—no, I could say with certainty we had not discussed any of that.

"Not even a little."

Wyatt's chuckle was mirthless as his gaze darkened to one of loss and pain and a fair bit of rage. "Nico killed Tomás the day you were taken. I wasn't there to see it, but I heard the stories. Nic was hurt bad by that Fae fucker, the bastard nearly crushed his skull just to get away clean. Catia sent the boys out so they didn't lose the scent trail, but Tomás? Well, even though he was in a cell half-dead from a challenge, he was still able to call his sons back."

I could see where this was going, and Wyatt didn't disappoint.

"As soon as Nico woke up and found out, it was all she wrote for Tomás. He ripped his wolf from him." Wyatt tipped his chin to Ghost. "And then tore out his throat."

Ghost was Tomás' wolf? Nico killed his dad? What the fuck?

Not Tomás' wolf. Am own wolf. Never owned. And Tomás was not worthy of me as his animal. The Alpha freed me.

I gulped, staring at the white wolf with its golden eyes and regal features. Nico was able to take an Alpha's wolf from him. He could command the liminal spaces for himself if he wished. I wondered if that was something I gave him with our bond or if he had that all on his own. Or what if it was both?

Spirit Alpha, Ghost supplied. *A ruler of the in-between. Like you.*

Shit. Ghost had tapped into my thoughts, and that was not at all comforting.

"Six months later, Nico found me. I was chained to a wall in that illusion mage's home. Starving, beaten, bloody, half-dead."

I covered my mouth, the sheer awfulness filling me. "I knew the illusion was too good. They took you, picked your brain clean. Oh, gods. Are you..." This time it was my laugh that was mirthless. "I was about to ask if you were okay, but... Okay is an illusion, too, isn't it?"

His mouth tipped up on one side. "It sure is."

Guilt hit me then, hurting my heart in a way I had yet to feel when my own family was killed right in front of me. "I'm sorry, Wyatt," I whispered, the pain of it all ripping me wide open. "I'm sorry they took you. I'm sorry they hurt you. I'm sorry they used you to get to me."

Swallowing it down, I reached my hand out and caught his. I couldn't do much, but I could heal him like I had Fiona. I could take away the pain in his joints and the ache he had in his lungs every time he took a breath. I could help.

Even if it wasn't enough.

Because the shit I couldn't take away was the real problem. I couldn't strip the memories from him. I couldn't give him six months of his life back. I couldn't take away the feeling of being used.

But I could help on the revenge front. "I take it the illusion mage is dead?"

Wyatt's smile was pure malice. "*They* are."

I tried and failed to feel sorry for Penelope Lewis. Her life had been stolen from her. She'd lost years of it and came back a shell of herself. But if she helped her father hold Wyatt captive for six months, whatever she got was too nice.

"But the Fae Prince. He's still alive, I'd bet."

Wyatt jerked a rage-filled nod.

"What do you say we find him?" I asked, knowing full well that Nico would throw a monkey shit fit if he even thought I was planning this.

His eyes narrowed as his "good old boy" face morphed into the meanest, "Don't fuck with me" mask.

"I'm in."

I knew my day would go sideways as soon as I opened my eyes.

For one, I woke up to a cold mattress and a note instead of my wife when she damn well knew to wake me. And two, Wren wasn't downstairs like she said she would be.

No, downstairs would have been a luxury. Downstairs would have been the height of perfection. Downstairs would have kept my heart from beating out of my chest and the contents of my stomach firmly in my gut.

Because my wife was outside barefoot in the middle of a sigil burned into the back lawn, speaking a language I could only guess was a Fae dialect.

Not exactly the way I wanted to wake up, maybe ever.

I had half a mind to march through that circle and snatch her ass out of it. Just as I was about to do just that, two pairs of hands stopped me. Wyatt and Theo shook their heads and pointed upward.

Suspended midair was Tristan—or rather, Drystan Haldrir Shadowfall, Crown Prince of the Dark Court. A coating of blackness held his arms and legs immobile while another snake of black fire collared his neck. Tristan gulped for air like a fish out of water, and then all at once, he fell to the ground, his bonds pulling at his limbs as if he were being stretched by four invisible horses.

After four months, the Fae seemed a hell of a lot better than I'd have thought he'd be. There was no getting out of Savannah—not without a damn good ABI deal under his belt and I seriously doubted he'd get one of those. The ABI was notorious for not dealing with the Fae as a rule. Plus, I'd passed along his information to Erica. My old boss had disseminated his likeness to every boundary agent. There was no getting out of here.

Not for him.

Still, he was dressed in clean clothes, and though his cheeks were sharp and his scars bright, he seemed better off than he should.

"Now, Drystan—you don't mind if I call you by the name your mama gave you, now, do you?" At his stoic silence, Wren carried on. "Well, Áine and I go way back —all the way to my childhood when she helped me come home. Gave me blessings and everything. She's also the one who helped me out of the Dark Court this time."

Wren clucked her tongue, her voice carrying a thicker accent as she let him know just how much he'd fucked up.

"You see, me being there is not a good idea. If it isn't your daddy hating me, well, my mere presence seems to cause a problem with the fabric of reality as we know it. As in, me being in the Fae realm doesn't just destroy the Dark Court—like I suspect you knew it would—it breaks the Seelie Court as well."

Oh. Oh, shit.

That got Tristan's attention. "My mother. Is she all right?"

Rage boiled in my belly, and it took everything I had not to find an iron blade and cut his fucking head off. Wren would have died because of him. She would have just... just...

"You selfish fuck," I growled, nearly losing the hold on my animal. "Is that all you care about?"

The Fae's gaze met mine. "Is not your wife all you cared about? She is my family. Why is that any different?"

Heat washed over me, and if I hadn't known better, I would have thought a flame could bloom on my skin just as it had on Wren's. "Because my wife was helpless against you."

Tristan raised an eyebrow. "Well, she's not helpless now."

No. No, she wasn't. That didn't mean shit, though. Wren didn't deserve any of this. *We* didn't deserve any of this.

"No, sweet pea, I'm not. But I do need your help, so I'll offer you an exchange." Wren snapped her fingers, the bonds around Tristan's neck and wrists and ankles melting away. "You help me open the Fae gates worldwide, and I promise to never summon you again. No torture, no pain, no grudges."

"Speak for yourself," Wyatt and I said at the same time.

Wren raised an eyebrow. "Yeah, but he isn't scared of you, now, is he? He's scared of me. Because he knows I could rip him limb from limb and make it stick. Or I could call on a Prince of Hell to haul his dumb ass on down to have a chat. Mr. Tristan thinks I am a destroyer of worlds, and while I can be, I have no interest in that particular pastime."

She focused on Tristan, her expression just a touch wrong as she leveled him with her sweetest smile. "Now do we have a deal, sugar plum, or am I going to have to get creative with my incentive? I guarantee I am meaner than my husband. I'll make what your daddy did to you look like fucking Disneyland."

Her eyes lit with twin flames, her green-gold irises changing to orange so fast it scared the shit out of me. She was bluffing. Or at least I hoped she was bluffing.

"Tik tock, Tinkerbell. I have problems to solve."

Tristan's gaze scanned the yard, which was full of my brothers and sisters and the majority of the pack. It stuttered on someone before moving away.

"Fine." He stepped closer to Wren, his voice going low, but I still heard: "I will help you open the gates, but you know what will happen. You know what he'll do."

Somehow between him taking his first step and his last word, I had his throat in my hand and his feet off the ground. I'd crossed Wren's circle and latched onto him so fast no one could have stopped me. And as much as I would have loved to squeeze the life out of him, I didn't.

Barely.

"You so much as look at her wrong and I will make sure whatever punishment she dreams up a reality. I know you don't care about pain, so I'll use my imagination."

Tristan's smug smile made me want to smash his

face in with my boot. "You could try, wolf, but your bride is correct. I fear her a lot more than I fear you."

But he didn't know what hope could do to a man. How it could make someone like me more ruthless than I had ever been.

"Let him down, Nico. He needs his voice if he wants to open the gates, and it's not like I can substitute him for another Fae. Trust me—I checked."

I nearly ground my molars to dust, but I released that fuck-wad and backed up a step. "Sure thing, Bird."

Did it matter that I was irrationally angry that she had started this shit without me? Probably not. After the discussion we'd had last night, I sort of thought this plan was not something she could do on her own. That just showed me, now, didn't it?

And when this was all over, I would put her ass over my knee and spank it until she begged me to fuck her. When this was all over, I would make her delirious with pleasure until she understood that we were in this shit together. And then... Then we would be us. She'd cook and I'd do the dishes, and we would lead this pack, and I would have her smiles and her laughs and one day— when things were calmer, and the world wasn't a complete dumpster fire—maybe we'd have kids.

We'd never talked about it. I knew she was covered as far as birth control, but we'd never discussed if she even wanted kids. With a family like hers, it was always a good possibility that she didn't. And as much as I wanted them, if she didn't, I knew we were enough.

But the thought of her round with my child did something to me.

Later, asshole. You have a Fae Prince to deal with.

Tristan looked at his feet. "I can't open the Fae doors."

Wren laughed—her giggle sweet as if she thought he was adorable. "Of course you can't. You borrowed your father's magic to do it, didn't you? I bet with all his playthings, he didn't even notice when you siphoned it off of him. It didn't matter how much they tortured you, you were never opening those gates. Right?"

Tristan took a healthy step away from Wren. "How in the blue bloody fuck do you know that?"

Wren pointed to the delicate skin beside her eye. "I can see better this time around. I bet you wished I was still the naïve little child falling for illusion mage's tricks, now, don't you?"

His lips twisted. "It would certainly help." His sigh sounded like he was trying to let his soul escape before Wren got ahold of it. "Fine. Do you have a plan, or are our asses just swinging in the wind?"

"Of course I do. But we need a change of venue."

A single snap of her fingers, and we weren't in the

backyard anymore. No, we were in Chatham Square, its burning gate still going even four months later. But this time, the fire didn't so much as singe our skin. We were in the middle, sure, and the flames roared so loud I couldn't hear my own thoughts, but nothing touched us.

Our pack stayed on the edges of the Square, but Wren, Tristan, Ghost, and I were right next to the Hell gate as if she was waiting on something.

Wren sucked in a deep breath, and then it was as if all the fire in the entire square filled her lungs. The never-ending flames flickered and died, their heat melting away on the breeze. The Hell gate stood tall for all the world to see, but it wasn't on fire anymore.

But Wren seemed to be made of it. Flames danced in her eyes as her red hair failed to follow the rules of gravity, floating in the air in a nimbus cloud around her head. And that didn't even touch the fact that she was floating at eye level with Tristan.

Tristan, smartly, was ghostly pale, his shock and fear stamped all over him. "I—I... I'm sorry—"

Wren's head tilted as she studied him, latching onto his wrist in a grip that made him wince. "The spell, Prince. Before I lose my temper. I will lend you the power you need while I can."

The Fae swallowed hard, trying to pull out of Wren's

hold. "Trying" being the operative word. "You know what's coming. He'll cross over. There won't be anything I can do to stop him."

"You let us worry about your father," I growled. "Here she has a whole pack at her back and the whole of the ABI. There she had squat. We can handle it."

Tristan's fear reminded me of Theo—of him horrified at his will being taken away. At the pain and filthy feeling he had when he had to do things against every rule he ever made for himself.

Fuck.

I did not want to empathize with this shit stain—especially when gratitude seemed to be stamped all over his face.

With a nod of agreement, dark magic swirled up his arms and legs as his brown eyes went black. He spoke in a guttural language similar to what Wren and Fiona before her had used, but it had a different cadence, different rhythm.

And maybe that was the difference. Or maybe he had always been the key, and he knew he couldn't do it alone.

A vine-covered door shimmered into being amongst the still-smoking grass and ruined trees. Flowers bloomed on the vines, a bright spot of color in the midst of the blackness. But more than that, it was as if the world itself took a breath, as if someone had opened a window in a stuffy house and now the air flowed freely.

Tristan almost wilted as fear really hit him, the stink of it coating his skin like oil.

"You're not done," Wren snarled, her grip on him going from tight to crushing. "As payment for fixing your fuck-up and lending you my power, you will bring me the forty-three women that your father stole."

What? She was letting him go? After everything he'd done, Wren was going to trust that he would do what she asked and—

"What? No." Tristan yanked at his arm in her grip, but Wren didn't so much as budge. The smell of burning flesh hit my nose as Tristan fell to his knees, Wren's feet touching the ground for the first time in minutes.

"*Yes.* I can't go into the Fae realm without destroying it," she hissed, pulling Tristan to her in an iron grip I didn't even think I could break. "As much as I would love to watch your father get crushed beneath his absolute *cliché* of a castle, I need those women back more. You get them out, and we'll be square."

Tristan howled as a flame flickered over Wren's hand, only getting louder as her fire-like gaze grew brighter. "Fulfill this bargain, and no member of the Acosta pack will hunt you—even though you deserve it."

"That's a tall order, Bird."

Wren's fire eyes cut to me, the censure in them enough to make the words on my tongue dry up. Well, that and she decided to speak inside my head like Ghost sometimes did.

I have a plan. Just trust me, will ya?

Wren turned back to Tristan, pained tears filling his eyes as she continued to burn him. "Because you and I both know that you can't go back home. You were banished to the Dark Court with your father for a reason, and your father wants to secure his crown, so... Earth is the only realm that will accept you. Bring me my payment, and you will have nothing to worry about from our pack."

Her smile turned cold despite the flames that seemed at home in her skin.

"Don't? And I will make sure you never stop running. There will be no safe place to lay your head or rest. No one hiding you, no one making sure you stay alive, no one showing you an ounce of mercy. Understand?"

Tristan's gaze fell from Wren's to my pack and back to her.

"We will never stop hunting you—not until we take an iron blade to your neck, or worse, our pack brings you to me. Now, do we have a deal?"

The Fae Prince gritted his teeth but gave an emphatic nod.

"The words," I growled, knowing full well a Fae or a demon deal required consent. And I had a feeling my wife was a bit more demon than I'd originally thought.

"We have a deal," Tristan gasped. "I will bring back the forty-three women stolen from Earth by my father. If they live, I will bring them home or give you the bones of those that have passed. I will not kill them, deal with them, or cause any undue harm."

"Excellent."

Wren let go of his wrist, the skin not quite as charred as I'd thought it would be. Where her hand had been was a blackened brand of shapes and lines, forming an intricate sigil.

"What did you do to me?" he whispered as his trembling fingers reached for the burn.

Wren's lips tipped up. "Cemented our deal. The marks will go away once you have fulfilled our bargain, and they allow me to track you on any plane should you decide to break it. You will also have a chaperone."

At the snap of her fingers, Wyatt strode forward, cutting the distance with long purposeful strides that told me that he would take great pleasure in Tristan not even attempting to fulfill his deal.

But she was asking him to lose years of his life in the Fae realm. She was—

He wants this, she said in my mind, breaking me out of my hastily formed planning session to figure out how to get him out of this predicament. *It's how he can heal. There are things Wyatt needs to do for himself, and this is it.*

But I was his Alpha. I was supposed to protect him like my father never did. My father didn't so much as flinch when he got taken, didn't say a word, and he had to have known when he'd dropped off the map.

Wyatt slapped my shoulder. "Don't worry so much, Nic. You'll grow yourself an ulcer."

His smile was resolute but sad, that carefree calmness that he'd had all of our childhood long gone. I hadn't seen it since before he'd been taken, and I feared I'd never see it again.

"I'll get right on that."

Of course I would—right after he came back safe and sound and hopefully with that Fae's head on a spike.

Wyatt bent, giving Wren a hug and then petting Ghost. When he straightened, he was kitted out in armor and weapons, a little gift from my wife.

"Be right back," he said, striding for the door like a man on a mission. "Come on, Pixie Dust, we've got a job to do."

Tristan stared at his brand before meeting my wife's still-flaming gaze. "This will go away when I deliver them, yes? No tracking, no hidden spells, I'll just be free."

Wren tipped up her chin. "That's the deal, but I'll offer a word of warning. Should Wyatt not return, or return harmed in any way, we'll strike a brand-new deal —one that will leave your mother gutted in front of you after I cut your eyelids away so you can't even blink. Understand?"

Tristan's face went white as he shakily nodded. "Yes."

"Fabulous. Now, off you go."

And then I watched the Fae I hated—and my best friend—walk through the same fucking gate that had taken Wren from me for three years.

All before my first cup of coffee.

I was in deep shit.

If Nico's face was anything to go by, I would be in said shit until the end of time. His emotions—which had a baseline of livid since I'd made it home—were dialed more to "burn the world down" levels. Add to that the trickle of a nosebleed coming from the power usage, and I figured I was fucked.

And not in a good way.

Before anyone could see it, I wiped my nose and ducked my face out of sight. Summoning Tristan had been a wild hair of an idea, sure. Lending him power to open the Fae gates, though. That had been really stupid.

Stupid and necessary.

But now that I had, I had no idea how I was supposed to exorcise every human in Savannah, close the Hell gate, *and* potentially rally against a Fae King who could be coming through those doors at any second.

Nico latched onto my bicep, pulling me into him so he could whisper in my ear: "You're bleeding. Why the fuck are you bleeding, Wren?"

It reminded me so much of that time up in Blue Ridge when he'd scented my blood for the first time. I'd been walking for hours, and the boots I'd worn had cut my feet up so much I could have been permanently deformed if he hadn't helped me.

I met his gaze, his gold eyes glowing in the morning sunlight. Gods, he was just as beautiful today as he had been that night up on the mountain. A little scarred, a little scruffy, but he was so fucking sexy it nearly killed me.

But I didn't answer him, and that pissed him off.

"Take us back home, Wren. Snap your fingers and bring my pack home, and then you and I can have a conversation."

I gulped. "Is conversation code for something, or do I need to write a Will?"

My smart mouth was going to get my ass killed one of these days. I had spent all the bravado I had making sure Tristan had no other recourse but to do what I wanted. Now, I was at Nico's mercy, and I couldn't decide if that was a good or bad thing.

"Do it. Now."

If I didn't do this, Nico would know just how weak I was now. If he knew that, he would never go for what I needed to do next.

This was going to suck.

Drawing in a deep breath, I snapped my fingers again, shoving the lot of us through space and time back to the Acosta compound. Squawks of indignation sounded all around me as we landed, the complaints mixed with a healthy dose of fear.

I couldn't blame them. Who knew what I even was anymore? A witch? A demon? Something in between?

Zephyr had given me so much power, so much knowledge, it was as if the girl I used to be was gone. I knew too much, felt too much, saw too much.

And that little trickle from my nose? Well, now it was a full-on waterfall.

My only stroke of luck was that I'd made the smart decision to glamour myself before I yanked out of Nico's hold, marching through the house and straight to the library. If Nico was going to yell at me—and I had a feeling he most definitely would, then I needed a sound-proof room for him to do it in.

But as quickly as I was moving, Nico still caught up to me just as I reached the door.

"Where the fuck do you think you're going? This is—"

His words died a quick death when I turned the knob and pushed the door wide. "Someplace new. I needed a place to put all the Bannister knowledge. Now, no matter what happens, we have it."

No matter what. No matter if I don't make it. No matter if I fail. But I didn't share those thoughts, I managed to keep them to myself.

Growling, he yanked me through the door and slammed it shut behind us, rage and heat and awe filling his gut. "You're pouring blood, but I can't see it. Don't you dare glamour yourself against me, Bird."

Bird. If Nico was still calling me Bird, then there was hope to be had. It meant I hadn't destroyed everything we were by overstepping, by acting like the Alpha I most definitely was not.

Sighing, I dropped it, letting him see what I'd done to myself just getting those gods-forsaken gates open.

"Jesus, fuck, Bird. What did you do to yourself?"

My knees wobbled and I wilted to the floor to my ass, my hands holding onto the hardwood planks like I could fall off the world at any moment. Opening the gates had been in Zephyr's instructions, but the deal?

That was all me. I had a feeling casting the repercussions was biting me in the ass right about now.

Savannah was broken because of me. Tristan, Diana, they thought I was a destroyer. Maybe I was. But I was also a fixer. Okay, so I caused more problems than I fixed, but I—

I could do this.

"There's a restroom right past the third shelf on the left. Can you get me a towel a—"

Nico cupped my face and pressed his forehead against mine. Instantly, warmth filled me as the blood dried in my nose and the worst of the aches eased. But even with as much power as we shared, he couldn't touch all of it.

"Thank you," I breathed, latching onto his wrists. The thrum of his pulse vibrated through my fingers all the way to my own heart.

"It's not enough."

No, it wasn't. But I didn't have enough time.

"Stay here, you understand me? Do not move from this spot."

Nodding, I didn't have the heart to tell him I couldn't stand on my own two feet if he'd paid me. I didn't know how I was supposed to exorcise anyone in this damn town let alone close the Hell gate. And the sheer thought of fighting Desmond on my home turf sounded exhausting.

Because I knew without a shadow of a doubt in my mind that he was coming. The way Tristan had felt about it, his father was worse than the devil himself. Granted, the pompous asshole hadn't been able to touch me in the Fae realm, but I had a feeling that ship sailed as soon as I made it back home.

A moment later, Nico returned with a hand towel and wiped away the blood that coated my face and neck. His hand trembled as he did it, the scene likely reminding him of that last time we'd been in this room. Well, not exactly this room, but still.

"You have to keep yourself safe. You have to live." Gently, he cleaned my skin, not letting himself look me in the eye. "I can't make it in a world where you don't exist, you hear me? I did it for three years and I... I... just can't do it anymore. Not without you."

"Nico," I breathed, but he cut me off with a violent shake to his head.

"Not without you, Bird. Before there was hope. Hope that you'd come back. Hope that you were out there somewhere safe. Hope that one day I'd see you again."

My heart was splintering into a million pieces in my chest at what he must have gone through. Because I knew exactly what too much hope could do to a person.

"It was the only thing that kept me moving, day in and day out for three years. It was the only thing that kept me breathing. If I lose you, I won't have that back. I'll never have anything close to it again."

I swallowed hard, the grief that he held in a tight little ball in his gut, the longing, the fear, it filled me in a way that I had never felt before. He was finally letting me in, finally letting me see just how much these last three years had scarred him.

"So you have to live, Bird. Whatever it is you have planned, I need you to remember that if you die, I die. If you fail, I fail. Because as much as I care about my pack, as much as I love them, I love you more."

What else could I say to that?

"I love you, Nico. I don't know what you survived to be here with me, but I'll thank every god if I have to." I ran my fingers through his long, wavy hair. It hung loose around his shoulders, the color mingling with his black shirt. "And I'll do everything I can to stay right here with you."

But I didn't promise I would stay alive—I couldn't—and he seemed to realize it.

Before I knew it, I was up and in his arms, my legs around his waist as he carried me to one of the tables. Knocking a stack of books to the floor, he set me on the edge. The way he looked at me, I might as well have been naked. It was as if he could see every inch of my skin, every freckle. Hell, he could probably see the way my nipples tightened and my sex clenched, both practically begging for his touch.

He hadn't even kissed me, and yet it was as if he'd marked every millimeter with his teeth.

Frozen, all I could do was let him look at me. All I could do was let him unbutton my top and spread it wide. There was nothing else but allowing him to peel the fabric from my skin, piece by piece until I was bare for him. I loved being exposed like this so he could feast on me with his eyes, that hungry gaze like a physical touch.

"As soon as I woke up this morning, I knew I was going to spank your ass today."

Fuck.

My sex clenched around nothing as I sat impatiently, squeezing my thighs together in an effort to control the ache. I remembered the first time Nico had spanked me. It was a lesson on who he belonged to—who I belonged to. I'd tried teasing him, and it had backfired in the absolute best way possible.

Without warning, Nico latched onto my hips and yanked me to the edge of the table before spinning me until my feet were on the floor and my ass was bare to him. The cool wood kissed my hard nipples as I scrabbled for purchase. But the first crack to my ass came before I was ready, the sharp sting so fucking good it had me rocking up on my toes.

"I told you to wake me if you left my bed, Little Bird."

The heat of him at my back, curling over me to whisper in my ear? Fucking marvelous.

Another crack against the opposite cheek had me moaning, and that was before his thick fingers played with the slick wetness between my thighs.

"You going to leave it again without me?"

I couldn't think of the right answer. On the one hand, I wanted his cock inside me, and if I answered in the affirmative, he'd most likely give it to me.

Oh, but if I hesitated, if I played stubborn, he'd play with me some more, spank me more, let the raw power that coursed through his very being wash over me. And *then* he'd fuck me until I couldn't walk.

Decisions, decisions.

"I don't hear an answer, Bird. Am I going to have to fuck it out of you?"

His hand cracked against my thigh right next to my pussy and the heat had me moaning again, which was the only answer he was going to get.

A second later, his cock was at my opening, the rough kiss of his jeans against the now-hot, over-sensitized skin a thing of beauty. And then he pushed inside, every single inch of him filling me so full I could hardly breathe. Nico's hand fisted in my hair, yanking me vertical as his other hand gently wrapped around my throat.

He didn't squeeze. It was more that he was reassuring himself in the space that I was breathing, I was alive, and he was, too.

"You're not leaving me," he growled against my lips. "Say it."

I wanted him to move—needed it—and I knew without a shadow of a doubt in my mind, he'd stay right there until I gave him exactly what he wanted.

He circled his hips, teasing me into near mindlessness.

"Say it, Bird, and I'll fuck you so good. I'll fill you so full. I'll make you scream. Tell me what I want to hear, and I'll do anything you want me to do."

His hand left my hair and encircled my wrists, damn near bending me in half as he continued to torment me —refusing to offer the friction I so desperately needed.

"Yes," I choked out, my greedy moan twisting my voice until it was almost unrecognizable.

Nico's grip tightened on my wrists as his one on my throat softened. He turned my chin with the softest touch, nipping at my bottom lip. "Yes, what?"

"I'll never leave your bed."

That earned me a delicious thrust of his hips that had me clenching to hold onto him. "What else?"

"I'll never leave you," I promised, and the truth of it was, I wouldn't. I couldn't. Death couldn't drag me away.

"That's my good girl." He let my wrists go as he kissed me until he had to hold me up. "Now hold onto something."

My hands scrabbled for purchase on the table, but just like the last time, I wasn't ready.

Nico fucked me like a man possessed. He fucked me so good I saw stars, whole universes, the heavens itself. He turned me, nearly bending me in half as he took out every ounce of his frustration, of his fear, on me, and I loved each and every minute of it. He kissed me until neither of us could breathe.

And when his fangs struck, I knew I'd keep my promise or die trying.

"Are you sure about this, Bird?"

Wren was currently poring over a book in her brand-new library, her shirt unbuttoned and hanging open to reveal her bra and miles of smooth, pale skin. While I appreciated the view, there was something to the frantic way she skimmed the book that had me sitting up and taking notice.

And no, I was not talking about my dick.

Wren creating this library for herself was a stroke of genius, one that felt like a slap in the face to my father. She had never gotten her revenge for what had transpired here, but taking this place and making it hers? That was masterful.

She waffled her hand at me while she turned the pages. "Yes and no. I need power. I used almost everything Zephyr gave me fixing what Tinkerbell broke. If I want to exorcise a whole fucking city without killing everyone, I'm going to need more juice."

She swiped the pages until she let out a *whoop* of joy. "There it is. Liminal spaces. Ghost said something to me earlier that got me thinking. He called you a Spirit Alpha, a ruler of the in-between. He said I, too, ruled that space. Now, I don't quite know what that means outside of liminal spaces."

Funny, I had been with that asshole wolf for three fucking years and now he was spilling his guts? He hadn't said a fucking word about this shit to me. Not one.

"Liminal space includes but aren't limited to, pocket worlds, Fae dimensions, the In-Between, and ancestral wells."

I didn't know dick about pocket worlds or the In-Between, but ancestral wells I knew enough about. And more often than not, they ran dry quick. Witches used them—especially ones that practiced ancestral magic. When a witch died, the family would bury them using a sacred ritual, allowing their power to fill the well. The problem was, witches didn't die every day, and the amount of power needed to sustain ones like the Bannisters was probably too much to keep magic flowing.

"Now the problem is, I have no idea if my family knew about the well, or if that was why they were killing off coven witches to siphon from. But the only way to tell is to go to the family plot and start asking questions."

Had I not been sitting on the table beside her, I would have fallen on my ass. "And by asking questions, you mean?"

Wren piled her hair on top of her head and secured it into a messy bun. "Commune with the dead and pray they don't get handsy?"

Outside of grave talkers, there weren't many people who could talk to the dead. A rare subset of arcaners, I only knew of one, and even she wasn't a full-on grave talker. "You got a grave talker in your pocket and forget to tell me?"

Wren sighed. "No, but I was empowered by a Prince of Hell, so it's possible I can use that to my advantage." She blew a raspberry as she stared at the book. "It's the best I've got."

"And what happens if the well is dry—if there are no more Bannister witches to siphon from?"

Frowning, she slammed the book shut. "Then we'll cross that bridge when we come to it."

WHILE BONAVENTURE CEMETERY WAS THE MOST FAMOUS IN Savannah, the Bannisters had never once been interred there. Too common for their tastes, maybe, or maybe they just didn't want tourists tramping all over their dead. Savannah had more cemeteries than anywhere else, but the arcane ones weren't on any tourist map.

Hidden in a forgotten corner of Forsyth Park, the Bannisters built a place that couldn't be accessed by anyone not of arcane blood. The only reason we knew about it at all was due to the information download, courtesy of Zephyr. Given that Wren was the last living person with Bannister blood, only she could give us access to the last spot on the planet she might draw from.

No, that wasn't true. There were other liminal spaces, but Wren worried that by drawing on them might destroy what was left. I mean, technically, she could open a Fae door and suck it dry, but then Wyatt and the women he was trying to bring home might be forfeit. She could call on Death herself for access to the In-Between, but that was a shade too risky—even for her.

No, the Bannister Forsyth Crypt was our best shot, even if it was a long one.

Hidden behind three thick oak trees that seemed to be twisted together into one, the entrance refused to reveal itself without a drop of blood from the pair of us. Only then did the trees untwist, unveiling a small meadow and a sprawling crypt with a spire that reached for the sky.

I had a bad feeling about crossing this boundary, but unless Wren wanted to burn herself out trying to exorcise all of Savannah, we were shit out of luck. Sacking up, I crossed first, making sure the place wasn't going to collapse on our heads or there wasn't a small pocket of rogue Bannisters waiting to kill us.

Only then did I beckon for Wren to follow me, my unease growing by the second.

Wren and Ghost crossed together, the damn wolf not leaving her side for a single moment since we left the library. He wouldn't say why, either, only that he was coming with us. Since Wren's return he had been stuck to her like glue, and while a modicum of jealousy hit me every time he wasn't at my side, it was replaced by the sheer relief that someone, somewhere, was always watching out for her.

As soon as Wren's foot touched down, the whole of the ground trembled, not easing my fears one bit. But then the air seemed to sigh as if it was happy someone was coming to visit.

Wren's gaze went wide as she whipped her head this way and that as if she could see shit I absolutely could not.

"What is it, Bird?"

She swallowed hard, putting her trembling hand in mine. "Either Zephyr scrambled my brain a bit when he worked his mojo, or I'm looking at a shit-ton of ghosts."

The trees shivered as a tinkling bell of a laugh shimmered on the breeze. *Oh, shit.*

Cold dread yanked at my stomach, and I tugged Wren behind me, backing up toward the entrance. Only... the trees moved of their own accord, twisting once more so that the entrance was just *gone.*

Fuck.

There was a small list of shit I was afraid of in this world. At the very top of that list was anything at all to do with ghosts. They were just a portion of the arcane that was outside of my wheelhouse. I couldn't see them, I couldn't fight them, and if they decided to be mean enough, they could rock your shit until you were a stain on the floor.

Ghosts were assholes.

And my wife could see them.

"Here," she said, forcing some of her power into me —power she absolutely could not afford to lose.

But then I saw. I saw and I wished I hadn't. Because it wasn't one or two or even a solid gaggle of five. No, that was a number I could work with. What fit into this small meadow was a gods-damned horde of ghosts.

And every single one of them was staring at Wren.

Did I say fuck? Because I meant fuuuuuuucccccccckkkkk.

But it wasn't like I could rip a ghost's throat out so unless these people were friendly, we were on the losing end of the stick here.

Their voices thrummed through the air like a swarm of bees, the see-through people buzzing with whispers as they talked amongst themselves. Some of them nodded and then a woman older than time made her way to the front. Even dead, she walked with a limp. I kind of figured ghosts would glide or something, but see-through and grayed-out, she hobbled forward until she was so close to us, I could almost scent her.

"Why have you come to us, child? Do you seek the well?" The old woman tilted her head to the side.

Slowly, Wren nodded before bowing at the waist. "Yes, Great mother, I wish to seek the power of the well. If it pleases you."

Her cadence was off, as if she was remembering a script at the last second, but I was still stuck on how fucking full this place was. I'd never heard of a well this stocked—not that I'd dealt too much with this side of the arcane.

"And you bring non-witches with you? In our sacred space?" It wasn't a chastisement, only an observation—or at least it was phrased like one.

Wren straightened. "With me is my husband, the Spirit Alpha of the Acosta pack, as well as a soul-ripped wolf. They are here as my protection, and I will not cast them from this space. They are family, and they are granted all rights afforded as such."

"Very well, if you feel you need your *protection*, you may have it."

Wren's gaze narrowed, and I could tell this was about to get real disrespectful real quick. "I wasn't asking."

The old woman smiled as if she'd said something funny, but I knew that Wren could only handle so much bullshit before she lost her shit, and this woman was already on her last nerve.

"If you do not wish to ask for our protection, why is it that you come to us? And so young? Why not consult an elder for what it is you seek?"

Wren's smile was as rueful as it was cold. "There is no one else. And I do not need your counsel. I need your power. All of it."

The buzzing intensified as the souls gossiped like old biddies. The ancient one's gaze seemed to really focus on Wren, a touch of fear there.

"I am the last witch of Bannister blood. The last born of our name. I will not birth a witch of our name, nor will any witch from my loins call upon this well. If you do not wish to help me, you will stay here. You will have no one to call upon you. You will have no one to receive your blessings. And you will remain here until the world ends and Death finally comes for what's left of you."

The ghost squawked, straightening as if Wren just told her to go fuck herself.

"But," Wren said holding up a single finger, "if you help me now, I will release you from the well so you may move on. You will find peace."

Avarice flitted through the woman's expression as the buzzing only got louder. "And what makes you think, child, that *we* need *your* help?"

Yep, this had the potential to turn real shitty real fucking fast if Wren didn't get them on our side.

Flames lit Wren's eyes as she stepped closer to the ghost before she blinked, and her irises returned to their normal green-gold. And even though that ghost was deader than a doornail, she backed up as if Wren could kill her twice.

"As someone who has been used for my power, I know exactly what help you need. You may want to feel some sort of honor in this, but you and I both know that you're trapped. You and I both know that you're bored and restless and release is the kindest thing I can do for you."

"You... you..." the woman gasped, still backing up. "*Demon.*"

Wren waggled her hand. "Not exactly. My mother made a demon deal while I was in utero. The demon thought my mother would abuse the power, so I got it."

The woman gasped again, only this time it was in shame. "Your mother is Margot Bannister."

"*Was*, yes."

The woman sighed again, her expression gaining more and more understanding as time went on. "And Eloise is your grandmother, Rupert, your father."

Wren nodded. "You refused her request for power, I take it? And Eloise and Judith, and any other slimy, worthless asshole in the line. Is that why there are so many of you left? Because Eloise destroyed everything the Bannisters used to be?"

"We would not let her gain an ounce of the power she sought. She wished to drain us dry to make herself Queen of this city, to destroy any other arcaner who stood in her way. Margot was delusional and too full of herself. They were not under attack. There was no war. But she was just like her mother—my daughter. Too much for my liking."

So, this was Wren's great-grandmother. Definitely not the oldest ghost in this place, but not the youngest, either.

"Eloise was nothing like her sisters. Where my other daughters were kind and trustworthy, Eloise only wanted more. More power, more money, more influence. I would not let her come to the well, and eventually, I put a spell on it so that she could not gain access. In time, she killed us, one by one. Either it was accidents or in-fighting or other arcaners, but I knew it was her. Soon, her daughter petitioned the well."

And because Margot was Eloise-lite, they said no, tipping this whole thing into motion. It was hard to tell if she'd done the right thing. If she hadn't, Wren wouldn't be the woman she was today, but if she had, Margot would have run this city into the ground decades ago. Wren might not have been born. We might never have met.

If Margot hadn't needed her, Wren's mother might have killed her or cast her out or...

"I don't blame you for telling her no," Wren murmured, staring at her feet. "You did the right thing.

But now I need your help, and I hope you see me without the stain of my parents."

"Tell us why you need the power, child," a man said, stepping forward. Dressed in turn-of-the-century garb—and by century, I meant the eighteenth—he seemed older than most here. "Tell us and we will decide."

"A Hell gate was opened in Savannah. I wish to exorcise the humans it has infected and close the gate. Also, a dark king from the Fae realm seeks to kill me and mine. I wish to protect them as best I can for as long as I can."

He studied Wren. "You do not seek status or money or fame?"

Wren looked at me and then back at them. "I don't need any of that. Hell, I don't even want any of that."

Too bad she already had most of those things. She had status as my wife and on her own as an ABI agent—if she still wanted to do the job. She had money because I had money. Plus, whatever was in the Bannister coffers was hers now. And fame? No one truly wanted fame. They only wanted the privileges fame afforded them.

"You only wish to help the city become one again?"

Wren raised an eyebrow. "That's what I said, isn't it? You want it written in blood or something?"

The man smiled before grasping the ancient

woman's hand. "No need. We can see inside your soul, child. We see past the words and into the marrow. We will give it all to you, and we will be free."

I kind of figured the deliberation would have lasted longer, but...

The horde shimmered into a swath of gold, fading slightly on the wind before moving in a massive murmuration right at Wren. It faded into her skin, filling her full of magic before my very eyes.

It was only then that I felt the slightest bit of hope.

But if anyone knew what hope could do to a man, it was me.

Being ready was an illusion.

Because there was no way to gauge just how ready one had to be to exorcise a whole city full of people. Or close a gate straight to Hell. Or not kill everyone while I did both.

Did I have enough power? Maybe. Was I prepared with spells and potions and odds and ends? Sure. Did I have that first clue of what I was actually doing?

Absolutely fucking not.

"Tell me again what Erica said when you called her?" I asked Nico as I stuffed a stasis potion bomb into my satchel. If I could, I'd wear a bandolier of them like an old-West gunslinger.

Fiona and I had been working on them all day. Those and black salt vials and iron ferrite bombs and blessed salt charges and anything else we could think of to cover our asses. Malia tried to help, too, but she said everything I touched was like grabbing onto a live wire even with gloves on.

A part of me hoped I'd go back to regular-powered Wren when this was all over. Because while I enjoyed being a badass, I missed just being able to hug my friends without zinging them into oblivion. The only person who didn't seem affected was Nico, which was a blessing all by itself.

Nico sighed before stilling my hand. "That the ABI couldn't get involved. While she wants to help, they are having a hard time securing the border. Too many months without news has made the rest of the region unstable. The ABI is dealing with a power-grab situation. It's not the first time and it won't be the last, but it looks like we're on our own."

Perfect.

The Acosta pack was large, but it was split almost in two after the Hell gate fiasco. The ABI cut off most of the city from the rest of the state, but a decent number of the pack was outside the limit. We had fifty fighters that were of age, not caring for an underage loved one, and capable of battle.

Fifty.

Against a city full of demons.

Like I said. Perfect.

I'd sort of hoped the ABI would *want* to back us up. I mean, we were solving a huge problem for them. Sure, it was a problem that we created—sort of—but a major one, nonetheless.

Nico's arm wrapped around my shoulders, and he pulled me into him. "Bird, don't you know that one wolf is worth at least ten fighters?"

Against demons?

Evidently the skepticism was stamped all over my face because Nico tipped his head back and let out a huge belly laugh. I would never get tired of that sound. His laugh lightened his features and took years off his shoulders.

"Don't worry, Bird. We'll handle this. Promise."

Yeah, we would. I just hoped we didn't get our asses handed to us before then.

By the time the pack was settled in Chatham Square, night had fallen in earnest. Without the constant flames, the din of the city was nearly gone, the silence almost peaceful if it weren't for the fact that we'd be calling roughly the entire city here in just a few minutes.

Okay, that was a complete exaggeration.

But incorporeal demons were the equivalent of fifty people. Each. And there were a fucking lot of them.

"Oh, come on," Hannah muttered, hip-checking me as she passed. "You faced down a death mage with no power at all. You can do this."

I finally broke my stare-down of the Hell gate to send her a skeptical side-eye. "That is an oversimplification, and you know it."

Fiona did the same on my other hip, only where Hannah was trying not to knock me over, Fiona put her whole ass into it. I stumbled a little before flicking her in the nose.

Before long I was giggling, which was likely the intended purpose.

"Oh, good," Malia said on a sigh. "Now I don't have to try and trip you or some other such bullshit to get you to settle down. No offense, Wren, but your power makes nuclear reactors look weak."

I winced, shrugging. "Sorry. But never fear. I'll probably blow the whole wad on the exorcisms and then you can relax. Speaking of relaxing, I was under the impression you'd be doing that instead of this?" I shot Fiona a glare. "You, too. What are y'all doing here?"

Fiona flicked me in the tender meat of my arm. "You know better, and how come you didn't ask Hannah that?"

Because I indeed *did* know better than to ask Hannah that question. She'd likely punt me into next week, Alpha's wife-slash-demon spawn or not. She was still pissed she didn't get to rip my family apart limb from limb and would not speak to Nico because he left her behind—not that it was his fault.

"Because I choose life?" I muttered, flicking her back.

Yes, we were acting like children, but dammit, I'd missed them. I knew it wasn't the same—to them I'd been gone for years—but having them around made life... better.

"Damn right she does," Hannah said under her breath, adjusting her weapons. On top of the axes Hannah had strapped to her back, she also had a satchel filled with as many potions as she could carry. Every one of us did, but especially the few of us who couldn't shift.

The ones that could? Well, they had a small arsenal, but they'd be using claws and teeth more than potion bombs. Before we'd come out here, Nico had made a new rule—one I approved of more than I could say.

Both parents could not fight together if they had

children underage. The families had to choose which parent to send—if any—so no child would be left orphaned. He also decreed that no one *had* to fight. He would not force them, and he would not take their will away.

He had more people fall to his feet in loyalty at that statement alone than Tomás had in nearly four hundred years. Wolves pushed back at the parent rule, asking to fight for him—for us.

But Nico wouldn't budge.

It made me proud of everyone who came to fight with us. Because this was family. This was loyalty. This was what I'd wanted my whole life. Now I had it and I prayed to every god, demon, and spirit that I could possibly think of that I didn't fuck it up.

Nico cut through the blackened square straight to me, his expression one of a determined Alpha. He was in his element, leading his people, and if I wasn't scared shitless I was about to accidentally napalm the entire city, I would have jumped his bones right then and there.

I mean, come the fuck on. How strong was I supposed to be against a full beard and his hair pulled back at the nape of his neck and that T-shirt stretched across his—

"You know I can feel that, right?" he whispered in my ear.

My eyes widened a little in faux surprise. "What? You're kidding. I had no idea."

His golden eyes melted me a little. They made me think I could do anything, and when he pressed a kiss to my lips, I almost believed it.

Almost.

Stuffing my fear down where emotions went to die, I managed a nod to signal I was ready. But before I could start the spell that would call the demons forth, I had one thing to say first.

"Thank you," I murmured, knowing every single one of them could hear me. "Thank you for being here with us, for being willing to fight. For showing up. I appreciate all of you." I cut a smile to Nico's older brother. "Even you, Theo."

He flipped me off and I blew him a kiss.

"You all embody what family means, and I will be forever grateful you accepted me into yours." Squeezing Nico's hand, I mouthed, "I love you" before walking into the biggest fucking witch circle I had ever made.

Only then did my chanting start.

I had to be careful with this part of the spell. If I used too much power, I wouldn't have enough left to exorcise the demons, but if I used too little, I wouldn't get them all. It was a delicate balance—a tight rope I was barely staying on.

One by one, possessed humans filtered through the carefully constructed wards at the perimeter of the square. It allowed the possessed in and no one out unless the wards were taken down from the inside. They wandered as if they were sleepwalking, bumping into each other, and stumbling over charred earth until they nearly reached the Hell gate.

There they waited, docile as a lamb, until I amassed almost more demons than the square could hold. Gulping, I quelled my chant, moving onto phase two of the plan.

Giving the signal, everyone readied their salt bombs while I did the completely asinine task of waking them up. There were too many to do the entire city at once, so batching them seemed like the best option.

Upset murmurings reminded me of talking to the ghosts of the Bannister ancestral well. The buzz was damn near deafening. I shot a pleading glance to Nico, and he let out a whistle so loud, dogs on the fucking moon covered their ears.

"Hey, everybody," I began from the center of my circle. "I know you're confused, but I need you to pay attention."

Fiona, in all her purple-haired glory, gestured to the

Hell gate while I continued my exit announcements like I was their damn cruise director or something. "This is the Hell gate. We are closing it tonight. If you wish to go home where it is warm, I need you to politely exit your host's body and pass through the gate immediately."

The demon closest to me practically clapped he was so happy. "Thank Deimos and all the torturers in Hell," he said, practically knocking me over with a feather. "Prince Zephyr told us we needed to stay here until you sent us home, and we cannot *wait* to get out of here. No offense, lady, but this place is freezing. I haven't been this cold since the Cubs won the World Series, and even then, Hell only froze over for twenty minutes, tops. I'm not allowed to kill anyone, I can't eat the animals, and the fresh meat selection is lacking."

Pressing my lips together, I tried not to lose it. This poor bastard had been stuck here just like I'd been stuck in the Fae realm, but his disposition was just...

"Umm... no offense taken?"

But reality set in quicker than lightning.

Why would Zephyr tell them to stay until I could send them home? Did that mean I didn't need to amass all this power? Did that mean I didn't have to fight?

As much as this was good news, I had a feeling it was pretty fucking bad.

Was this another test? Or was it something more?

My confusion rattled down to everyone else, and Nico tensed at my side, moving closer to me, crowding me, totally going off script as far as the plan. I couldn't make myself give a shit.

"Did Zephyr say anything else?" Nico asked, his voice low and commanding, making the demon stand up straight. "Give you any other instruction?"

The demon frowned at him before cutting his gaze to me as if he were waiting to see if I was okay with him spilling the beans. I nodded, urging him on.

"It's okay. This is my husband and our pack. You can tell us."

The demon screwed up his mouth and stepped closer. Almost everyone tensed, but I met him at the boundary of my circle because I knew. I knew it was bad and he was going to tell me the worst.

"Zephyr said we had to take care of our hosts. Keep them fit and fed and clean. We couldn't destroy their lives in any way—which is rude. These people accepted us of their own free will—putting 'Welcome' signs everywhere. It was as if they were just asking to be possessed, and we couldn't do *anything*. It was actually quite opportune because not all of us could find a host and had to go back home."

"That's not—" I shook my head. "The 'Welcome' signs are meant for humans. Those are not blanket consent. Did anyone express their consent where your host said that you could possess them and not just a 'Welcome' sign? Raise your hands."

A decent pocket of people raised their hands, including the demon closest. Okay, so not a total takeover via cutsie welcome mats.

"But more, Prince Zephyr said that we must obey you. Protect you. He said a battle was coming and you would need the help."

It was as if the ground dropped under my feet. We needed to move this shit along, and fast.

I nodded, understanding hitting me square in the face. "Anyone who did not get express consent from your host or gained it using trickery, it is time to leave. Now. Go home to Hell, and thank you for caring for your hosts. Your job is done."

There was one such demon about ten feet away, and she gave me a grave nod before tilting her head back. Then she vomited an oily black smoke into the sky, her whole body shaking like she was being electrocuted. The black smoke headed for the gate, slipping into the seams of the door before winking out of sight.

One down...

The demon's host—a yoga-pants-wearing, mom-bun-having human crumpled to the ground on her hands and knees, coughing up what remained of the black sludge. Then one by one, the others followed suit, blotting out the full moon and all the stars with the incorporeal bodies of the demons on their way home. By the time it was all said and done, I had maybe thirty humans wondering how the fuck they'd gotten here.

That's where Fiona came in. With a wave of her hand, the bright-blue potion bottles surrounding the gathered demons exploded, their contents waving through the air as it sought out the non-possessed like heat-seeking missiles. The smoke collided with the humans, filling their noses, leaving them like mindless automatons.

"Go home, go to bed, remember nothing of this night. You will awake in the morning and go back to your life as you know it."

I'd heard of vampires being able to mind-control people, but vampires had been *persona non grata* in Savannah for centuries. When Fiona mentioned a potion that could replicate that same power, I knew it was the only way. Or at least, it was better than trying to mind-wipe them one by one with my untested magic.

The group moved in different directions, heading to wherever they called home.

This was good, so why did it feel like it was about to bite me in the ass?

This wasn't right.

Zephyr had set this up so we had an army at the gate. So, what did he think was about to come through that we'd need a whole pack and a gaggle of possessed humans at the ready?

And how did he know to send them through in the first place?

Everyone, move to the Fae gates. Be ready.

My command shimmered through the pack as many set down their salt bombs to shift to their animals. Wolves were better prepared for battle in their animal skins than in human form, anyway. And it looked like the salt bombs were probably the most unnecessary endeavor we'd done in the last twenty-four hours.

I had a feeling we'd need those iron ferrite ones a fuck of a lot more.

"I don't like this," Theo said, moving closer to our circle.

I didn't, either. "Fi, call the rest of the demons. Fuck the batching shit. Get them all here. Now."

"On it," she replied, nodding as if she was just about to do that very thing. "You might want to put out a call to our ABI buddies. Demon-possessed humans aren't exactly the top of the food chain."

Wren jerked her chin in the affirmative before waving her hands in an intricate dance. Cell phone towers had been down since the Hell gate opened, as well as most Internet access. Wren's little hand-waving was the only way to get a long-distance message out.

"She might get wigged out by the mental download," Wren said, shrugging, "but it got the job done."

I reached for her, wanting to pull her behind me, wanting to get her the fuck out of here, wanting just once for her to be safe and sound with no one and nothing trying to kill us. Her fingers found mine and then the whole world seemed to tilt.

The ground pitched, roiling beneath our feet as all those demons poured right back out of the Hell gate. Blacking out the sky, they screamed past us, shouting warnings that none of us could hear.

The door burst wide as the flames ignited once again, and out came scores of Fae, but none of us were paying attention to the smaller offerings from the Fae realm. They didn't seem to want to be here at all. No, we were looking at the tall man with the bone crown waltzing onto our plane like he had any right to be here.

Desmond.

Like most Fae, he had a long fall of hair, his the blackest of midnight with the same sharp features his son had. But while his son was tall, Desmond was taller, thinner, and power seemed to roll off him in waves.

Wren had said he hadn't been able to touch her in the Fae realm—that according to the Seelie Queen, no Fae could. But given that the Fae at Ellie's house had picked her up with no problem—that they struck her and tried to take what was mine—that reprieve was over.

Desmond scanned the crowd of shifters and demons and his amassed army of Fae before he landed on my wife. I had the strongest urge to fly across this circle. To put my sword in his gut and split him open.

His mouth stretched wide in what could have been a smile, delight hitting his eyes. He'd come for her, and he'd get her over my cold, dead corpse.

"Wren Bannister," the fucker simpered, his smile a

touch too big for his face, his sharp white teeth too large for his mouth. "I've been looking for you."

"Funny," Wren shot back, "I was sort of hoping you'd have fallen off a cliff by now and drowned in your own blood." She pulled a sharp dagger from the sheath at her hip as she drew Fiona, Hannah, and Malia back with her magic, placing them inside the circle with us. "Looks like neither of us are getting what we want."

Wren stabbed the earth with her blade and a circle of golden magic drew up from the ground like a shield. "You couldn't touch me there and you sure as shit can't touch me here. So whatever throne you want, you're not getting it."

Desmond sauntered forward and put a single finger to Wren's ward. His finger sizzled but he didn't so much as flinch. "I was hoping for more power from you. What with your parentage and demon lineage and all. Pity. But the pack you provided and the demons just lying about? Well, they might just do the trick. I'll even take your husband this time. Had I known you were mated to a Spirit Alpha, I would have had my son steal you both."

Be ready to shift, Wren's voice screamed across my thoughts. *Make sure the pack is ready.*

But the pack was already shifting, jumping to their wolves as quick as a blink while Ghost was gearing up to eat his weight in Fae.

Three... two... one.

Wren ripped the blade out of the earth and threw it, hitting the Fae right next to Desmond in the neck. This close to the open Fae gates, she'd insisted on using iron blades. Now I could have kissed her for thinking of it because that Fae dropped like a stone, catching Desmond off guard.

My wolf took over before I ever told him to, jumping to his form and leaping forward as the world erupted into battle.

"Protect the daughter of Zephyr," the demon closest to Wren cried into the night, and the rest obeyed, surrounding my wife in a wall of bodies.

Possessed humans didn't have a ton of magic, but they were better than nothing, and the incorporeal ones? Well, they were already wreaking havoc with the Fae around Desmond, choking them, blinding them, doing anything and everything they could to give us an advantage. But as much as they were doing, and the spells that were coming from Fiona, and the brute force of Hannah, and the claws and fangs of my pack...

Nothing touched Desmond.

Not even me.

I watched Nico jump before I could tell him to stop. Stuck behind more bodies than I cared to think about, there was no way I could have reached him in time.

No way I could have warned him.

Because I hadn't thrown that blade at just *any* Fae. I had thrown it directly at Desmond, and my aim had been true. But somehow nothing hit him, not one spell, not one blade. Nothing penetrated his defenses.

So when Nico jumped, all I could do was scream as Desmond's arm shot out, plucking Nico's wolf right out of the air like a flower in a garden. And just like with all his other playthings, he tossed my husband away from him like trash.

And even though I could feel Nico's heartbeat in my chest better than my own, even though I could feel the breath in his lungs, when he didn't get up, it still felt like I was dying. Like my soul was breaking apart piece by piece.

The scream that ripped from my throat had a power all on its own, casting demons and wolves and Fae alike away from me as if they had all been pulled by a string.

Zephyr. Please. Please come. Please help me. Help us. Please don't let me lose him.

The wealth of magic from the ancestral well roiled beneath my skin. I'd done a good job of cloaking it, but now was not the time to be modest. No, now was the time to rip that Fae fucker to shreds and dance on his innards while I bathed in his blood.

Or I could just kill him. Killing him would be good.

But it didn't matter what I threw, it just bounced off. Sure, those ricochets landed on the Fae surrounding him, but I didn't give a shit about those assholes.

I wanted the king.

The definition of insanity was doing the same thing over and over and expecting a different result. After tossing more power than I could afford to lose, wising up was my only option. If pushing didn't work, maybe pulling would.

So I drew him to me, reaching his ward and digging my fingers in it like I could bend the magic to my will. Desmond's smile—which had seemed so joyous before—trembled and fell.

"You think you can come here to my home and start wrecking shit? You think you can take and take and take and no one will put an end to your fuckery?" My fingers breached his ward, ripping it away like I wanted to do to his flesh. "You think you can hurt my family and I won't put your ass in the ground?"

"Stop, Wren," someone called but I couldn't focus on the fight around me.

Sure, I saw the demons ripping into the Fae, I knew the pack was taking their lickings and returning the favor. I felt Fiona using all she had to push against the horde Desmond had somehow called to us from all around Savannah.

I knew all this and still...

All I wanted was to know for certain that Nico was okay and to rip Desmond limb from fucking limb, and as long as I had those things, I would be happy as a clam.

But there was a flaw in my plan.

You see, when I ripped away Desmond's protection, I took away the barrier between us. Simple. Logical. But I wasn't logical right then. Because as soon as the magic floated away on the wind, the Fae King proved a theory.

He could most definitely touch me here.

And as the sharp slice of the blade cut through my belly, I knew for a fact what it was to lose. Because he wrapped his fingers around my throat, his icy skin making the dreaded knowledge worse. I had been so focused on revenge, so fixated on showing him that no one could hurt me, I'd let him far too close.

I'd handed him the winning ticket and he'd barely played the game.

"I knew hubris would do you in," Desmond murmured, his face too close to mine, his lips at my ear, his touch leeching the warmth from my very bones as the blood leaked from my belly.

"In my kingdom all you could do was taunt me. All you could do was insult my kingdom before stealing what I was promised. I think I'll make you beg me to kill you before I'm done."

"Fuck you. I'll never beg for you." Using what little strength I had left, I spat in his face, the blood-tinged saliva painting his skin red.

Then he dropped me just like he had all the others— just like he had Nico. Personally, I just figured the fuck wanted to stand over me, and if I could have moved my legs, I would have kicked him. But I was pretty sure he'd nicked my spinal cord with that fucking blade so moving said legs was out of the question.

So was breathing and walking and pretty much everything. I had been so stupid.

Nico. I'm so sorry.

A flash of red-stained white fur sailed over me headed straight for Desmond. Ghost bowled over the Fae King, his fangs tearing into his shoulder as the pair of them rolled. Desmond howled in pain as Ghost readjusted his grip, ripping the wound wide and damn near taking the whole arm off. Desmond's uninjured arm shot out, calling the blade that was still in my middle back to him.

Then that blade was in Ghost, tearing him open just like I was. The giant wolf yelped, staggering away as Desmond cradled his abused arm.

Ghost. My good beast. I'm so sorry.

I reached for him, only making contact with the blood that poured from his middle. Neither of us could move, and it wasn't enough. I hadn't done enough—I hadn't tried enough. I just wanted Savannah back the way it was, but maybe that was too much.

I should have played it smarter, should have consulted anyone else.

Am not good beast. Did not protect you. You're dying. We're dying.

Swallowing, tears ran into my hair as the pain bit

into me. *You're the best beast. You kept him from taking all the power. You did so good.*

So tired. Don't want to leave you.

The reality of it was too much. Nico was alive out there. He could heal him, right? He could do something.

Nico, Nico, Nico. Please, someone help us. Please. Zephyr, someone, please!

Nico's face appeared over mine along with Zephyr's, two more men next to him—all four with this odd golden halo around their bodies like they were angels or something. One was blond, the other dark haired. Princes. Brothers. I returned my focus on Nico, and the wolf under his skin stared at me, his gaze sad.

Help Ghost. Somebody help him. I messed up. I'm sorry.

"Jesus fucking Christ, Bird. What happened to you?" Tears swam in Nico's eyes as he cradled me to his chest. "Not again. Please, no, I can't do this again. Stay with me."

Help him. Help Ghost.

"We're losing them," Zephyr warned, scraping his fingers through my open middle before mixing it with Ghost's blood. "I—we—can help."

"I don't care what it costs," Nico growled, "or what favor you need. Whatever it is, do it. I'm not losing her again."

The two men and Zephyr locked gazes and nodded. Each one dipped their fingers in our mingled blood, drawing a rune with it into the side of their cheeks. Zephyr latched onto Nico.

"Sorry about this. It's gonna hurt."

At once, all three brothers snapped their fingers, and Ghost, Nico, and I all convulsed.

Don't want to leave you. I want to stay. Please let me stay. Ghost was ripping my heart in two, and that said nothing to the tearing ache in my whole body at Nico's scream.

But Nico was a Spirit Alpha. Maybe... *Maybe...*

Then Ghost melted into a pool of golden light, his fur, flesh, and blood just gone. As much as it hurt, as much as I couldn't move, none of that stopped the sobs that ripped through me.

I want to stay. I want to stay. I want to stay, he pleaded and the pain of it damn near killed me.

That pool of light reached for me, and I reached for it. It settled on me, filling me, healing me, merging with my very soul as Ghost's light crowded my heart and settled there. I felt myself stitch back together, and I took my first real breath in minutes.

Ghost?

Something stirred in the back of my mind, growing

larger with each passing second. A presence that hadn't been there before.

My queen?

It wasn't the same voice as Ghost had used before. It was lighter, younger, less masculine.

Ghost, is that you?

Ye-yes, my queen. I think so. I feel different but still me.

Trembling, I put a hand to my mouth, curling into Nico's warm embrace. "You saved him. You saved us."

Nico dropped kisses to my face in his relief. "Never again, you hear me? Don't you ever do that to me again."

Zephyr snorted. "Oh, I don't think you'll have to worry about that. Wren, my darling girl. You must shift. It's the only way to keep Ghost. You must cement the bond."

But I didn't know what that meant. Was Ghost part of me now? Was he my wolf? Was this what Nico felt when he said his wolf was speaking to him?

"I can help, but it must be your choice. Do you wish to keep Ghost with you?"

Of course I did. "Yes."

Zephyr smiled, breathing a sigh of relief. "Then you need to step back, Nico."

At his snap, it felt as if I was being squeezed through a soft portal, and then I wasn't on two feet but four.

"Holy shit," Nico breathed, his eyes wide. "That's not... She's a—"

Zephyr shushed him. Shaking myself, I stretched my shoulders, feeling an unfamiliar weight there. You know, it was probably better if I didn't see myself right away.

"What in the fucking dragon wolf is that?" Theo said, and I could only guess he was talking about me.

Ghost?

Zephyr and Aemon and Bael gave you pieces of themselves to save us. We look a bit different.

It seemed like I would be getting to a mirror soon enough, but first...

Desmond's Fae stink filled my nose and I found him trying to get away from the battle. Hannah had him by the ankle, his bone crushed in her hand as Fiona bombarded him with her magic. Flesh burned and screaming, he tried to claw away, but not from either of them. Malia held onto his head, her hands glowing as she poured something into him as he tried to bat her away with his one good arm.

"You like pain?" she snarled in his face. "This is all the pain you caused. Fucking choke on it."

I'd have felt sorry for him, but I damn near died, so my pity was shot for the time being. Desmond had taken so much from so many people.

A growl filled my—our—belly.

Ghost?

Lunch, my queen?

Yeah.

With the moon overhead and the battle still raging, it was lunchtime.

SIX MONTHS LATER

It took time to get used to the new normal and even more time for Wren to get used to shifting. For one, she wasn't a wolf—or at least she wasn't all wolf. Zephyr, along with his brothers Aemon and Bael, and I used our essence to merge Wren with Ghost. In doing so, it put little pieces of us in her, too.

The only place Wren could shift was up in the mountains in secluded spots and a few pockets of Savannah. Wolves were sneaky and could blend in. The midnight-blue, winged, scaled, fire-breathing smoke monster of a wolf that was now Wren's other form?

Not so much.

There wasn't a place in Savannah she could hide, except for a small clearing hidden from prying eyes, being three braided oaks at the back of Forsyth Park.

There, she learned to fly, learned to shift, learned to be.

But tonight was special in more ways than one.

A flame hot enough to melt a car shot into the sky, heating the cool air up a bit. It was winter in Savannah, and though that didn't mean much being so far south, the nip in the air was noticeable. That was one of many bonuses to the fire power that Wren now had.

That and she was damn near indestructible. Nothing could get past those scales, and if it did, well, she'd turn into smoke or fly away or... honestly, she could be a little scary if she wanted to be.

I fucking loved it.

A moment later, Wren stood on two feet, her jeans and sweater no worse for wear in the change. It irked me a little bit that shifting came so easy to her. It took me years before I figured out how to take clothes with me and even longer to figure out how to stay clothed when I came back.

Shifter houses made for a lot of accidentally naked people sometimes.

"Is it almost time?" she asked, cutting through what

had once been the Bannister ancestral well. There were no ghosts here anymore, but Wren still liked the place.

It still gave me the creeps.

"Yeah," I said, grabbing her hand in mine. "They'll be back in about an hour. You ready?"

Wyatt and Tristan were due back today, the information a gift from the Seelie Queen herself. She'd shown up about a week after the battle, quelling nerves and smoothing the rough edges of the aftermath.

Desmond was dead, and most of the Fae around town were celebrating. It was possible that there was no other choice but for them to be happy, and at the moment, I just didn't care. The Fae were now someone else's problem, and unless they made it mine, I was staying out of it.

Áine seemed to have the lot well in hand, but she would be going home soon and leaving her bastard of a son in charge. That was if he followed through with the deal he made, and Wren didn't eat him first.

"Yep. I just needed to get my wiggles out. Ghost was getting restless."

Wren was restless a lot these days.

Her ABI contract was still "processing," and until they got their heads out of their asses, Wren was in limbo. I understood the problem from both sides. She was an Alpha's mate, a brand-new shifter, and the product of a demon deal. Just one of those things disqualified her from service, but all three?

She was an insurance nightmare.

Wren just wanted her books cleared and to move on. With all she'd done for Savannah, you'd think someone higher up on the food chain would have gotten the lead out. But I had a feeling she wished she could do something that was just hers.

"Come on. I want to show you something."

We strode together through Forsyth down to the parking lot, and I took her to the one place I'd been dying to all day. If today went as planned, I knew the ABI would allow Wren to cancel her contract. With returning that many missing agents, it was a no-brainer. But Wren needed something all on her own.

And maybe she would want friends with her.

"Keep them closed, Bird. If you ruin this surprise…"

"Yeah, yeah, yeah. You'll turn me over your knee. If I've told you once, I've told you a thousand times. Quit threatening me with a good time."

Truth be told, I'd turn her over my knee just because she liked it, but I didn't want to spoil the surprise. I parked on Broad Street and guided her down the treacherous stairs that led to our first meeting. But unlike then, she didn't so much as stumble on the cobblestones.

"Why in high holy hell are you taking me down to the Walk tonight of all nights?"

"It's a surprise, woman."

Grumbling, she kept her eyes closed until we stopped at the very building that was now in her name and her name alone.

"Open them."

Azalea Apothecary had once held this very spot. After it burned down, another apothecary took its place, but the people of Savannah didn't take to it, putting it out of business. Now it was a new building, one that would likely stand the test of time.

Wren's green-gold eyes focused on the blue building, her gaze zeroing in on the sign. The white "Midnight Investigations" sign was brilliant against the midnight-blue paint, highlighting the name for all the world to see.

"I'd originally thought of Bird Investigations, but Fiona and Ellie vetoed it."

Wren's mouth opened and closed as hope bloomed in her expression.

"The building is yours. Just yours. The business is yours. You can tear it down or build it up, but I think what you love about the ABI can still be in your life, even—"

Wren's smile was a touch evil. "Even if they fire me tomorrow?"

I wrapped my index finger around her pinky. "Yeah. Plus, I wanted you to have something that was just yours."

"I love it. Plus, the ABI in this town leaves a lot to be desired—especially without its best agents. This is…" She sighed like the relief was just hitting her. "Perfect."

"Want to see inside?"

Giggling, Wren dragged me by the hand, unlocking the door with a snap of her fingers. She studied every nook and cranny, loving the reception desk and offices, but when she turned back to look at me, she found me on one knee.

I wasn't nervous. I'd been married to Wren in my mind for years. But it always irked me that in the confusion of our mating, I'd never really asked her.

"Wren Adelaide Acosta, will you be my wife?"

Her irises flashed gold. "I'm already your wife."

"Is that a yes then?"

"Ask me like you did the first time. I know what it means now."

I pulled the velvet box from my pocket, opening it to reveal the sapphire that now matched the color of her animal.

"Tell me you want this. Tell me you're mine. Tell me you want me."

"I do," she whispered, and that was all I needed to hear.

WE WERE MORE THAN A LITTLE LATE TO THE GATE AT Chatham Square. Okay, we were fifteen minutes late, rumpled, and a teensy bit fuck drunk, but luckily Wyatt and the motley crew were also running behind. Áine stood beside the door opposite my mother, Theo, Erica, and a small assortment of pack and Fae alike.

I'd had feelings about Erica and Áine being here, but they'd both insisted.

"Oh, good, right on time," Áine cooed, her smile not the least bit sarcastic. "I knew you'd be a little late today, so I padded the timeline a bit."

Nope, not touching that.

Three minutes later, the door that we'd been waiting six months to open creaked wide. Wyatt's blond head came out first, followed by a sea of women in various states of injury. Some walked of their own accord, and some were carried on makeshift stretchers.

Tristan was the last one out, carrying a small woman with no hair and as thin as a rail.

Erica whistled and a team of medics descended, escorting them away so they could be cared for, so they could regain their lives, so they could actually breathe. After the last woman was handed off, Tristan approached my wife, his forearm still burned.

"I've fulfilled your bargain," he snarled. "Take it off."

Wren's smile only served to piss him off. "To you it's been half a day. You wish to be free so soon? What if someone wanted to find you?"

Tristan waved his arm in front of her face. "Then they'd summon me themselves," he ground out. "Take it off."

She latched onto his arm, making Tristan's face pale. "You have brought me every missing woman?"

He gulped. "Yes."

Wyatt seemed no worse for wear, either. Considering Desmond was dead, the resistance at his castle had probably been nil.

"Very well." She let him go and snapped her fingers, the burn melting away instantly. "Talk to your mother. She misses you."

With that, the Fae contingent was dismissed. Erica met my eyes over the heads of my pack, her gaze landing on Wren and then flitting back to me. The ABI would let her go tomorrow with her years paid in full. Erica's gaze fell on Fiona as well. Erica knew all about who really opened the Hell gate, no matter what Zephyr passed it off as.

By the look on her face, someone else in the ABI might know as well.

But that was a problem for another day.

My pack was whole, Wren was safe, and soon things would finally calm down.

Eventually.

This concludes The Wrong Witch Series.
Thank you so much for reading. I can't express just how much I have adored writing Wren & Nico and their ragtag bunch of friends.

However, if you would love to see a special glimpse of Wren & Nico many years later, turn the page for an epic Wrong Witch Bonus Scene. I hope you enjoy it!

*If you loved Wren & Nico and would like to see more from the Acosta pack, stay tuned for **Curses & Chaos** and all the*

crazy, witchy shenanigans that is to come. I hope you're buckled in to see Fiona contend with the aftermath of her Hell gate snafu, life as a witchy mob princess, and her sinfully hot, totally clueless mate.

Want the skinny on future releases without having to follow me absolutely everywhere on social media?
Text "LEGION" to (844) 311-5791

BONUS SCENE

Dear Reader,

I hope you enjoyed The Wrong Witch Series. Wren & Nico have a very special place in my heart, and I am absolutely ecstatic for you to read more about them.

I have an extra special bonus scene for you as a thank you for reading. All you have to do is click the link below, sign up for my newsletter, and you'll get an email giving you access!

SIGN UP HERE:

https://geni.us/ee-bonus

CURSES & CHAOS

The Lost Witch Book One

If the ABI finds me, I'm dead.

Agent or not, when your dad is the head of the most notorious arcane crime family in the country, no one believes you when you say you didn't open that gate to Hell on purpose.

Now, I'm practically glued under enough null wards to hide a god and stuck with a stupidly sexy shifter of a jailer who hates my guts.

When my former employer comes sniffing around, not only does he keep me alive, but we find out that our pasts are far more connected than either of us realize.

And the lies we've been told could kill us both.

Read Now!

BOOKS BY ANNIE ANDERSON

SEVERED FLAMES

Ruined Wings

Stolen Embers

Broken Fates

IMMORTAL VICES & VIRTUES

HER MONSTROUS MATES

Bury Me

SHADOW SHIFTER BONDS

Shadow Me

THE ARCANE SOULS WORLD

GRAVE TALKER SERIES

Dead to Me

Dead & Gone

Dead Calm

Dead Shift

Dead Ahead

Dead Wrong

Dead & Buried

S OUL R EADER S ERIES

Night Watch

Death Watch

Grave Watch

T HE W RONG W ITCH S ERIES

Spells & Slip-ups

Magic & Mayhem

Errors & Exorcisms

T HE L OST W ITCH S ERIES

Curses & Chaos

Hexes & Hijinx

THE ETHEREAL WORLD

P HOENIX R ISING S ERIES
(Formerly the Ashes to Ashes Series)

Flame Kissed

Death Kissed

Fate Kissed

Shade Kissed

Sight Kissed

ROGUE ETHEREAL SERIES

Woman of Blood & Bone

Daughter of Souls & Silence

Lady of Madness & Moonlight

Sister of Embers & Echoes

Priestess of Storms & Stone

Queen of Fate & Fire

To stay up to date on all things Annie Anderson, get exclusive access to ARCs and giveaways, and be a member of a fun, positive, drama-free space, join The Legion!

facebook.com/groups/ThePhoenixLegion

Acknowledgments

A huge, honking thank you to Shawn, Barb, Jade, Angela, Heather, Kelly, and Erin. Thanks for the late-night calls, the endurance of my whining, the incessant plotting sessions, the wine runs... (*looking at you, Shawn.*)

Basically, thanks for putting up with my bullshit while I recovered and clawed my way out of post-surgery brain fog.

Every single one of you rock and I couldn't have done it without you.

ABOUT THE AUTHOR

Annie Anderson is the author of the international best-selling Rogue Ethereal series. A United States Air Force veteran, Annie pens fast-paced Urban Fantasy novels filled with strong, snarky heroines and a boatload of magic. When she takes a break from writing, she can be found binge-watching The Magicians, flirting with her husband, wrangling children, or bribing her cantankerous dogs to go on a walk.

To find out more about Annie and her books, visit www.annieande.com

facebook.com/AuthorAnnieAnderson

instagram.com/AnnieAnde

amazon.com/author/annieande

bookbub.com/authors/annie-anderson

goodreads.com/AnnieAnde

pinterest.com/annieande

tiktok.com/@authorannieanderson

www.ingramcontent.com/pod-product-compliance
Lightning Source LLC
Chambersburg PA
CBHW051126190726
48290CB00006B/1699